I have always sworn by the wisdom of travelling with companions. In dangerous situations, the more companions you have, the more secure you will feel.

And what about companions for that moment when you enter the Kingdom of Death? Well, let me put it to you this way: have you ever wanted the entire city of Vushta to be your friend?

— from SOME THOUGHTS ON APPRENTICESHIP
by Wuntvor, apprentice to Ebenezum, greatest
mage in the Western Kingdoms (a work in progress)

"A bizarre, witty, delightful fairy tale for grown-ups!"

— Mike Resnick, author of *Stalking the Dragon*

"A delightful, very funny, superbly off-the-wall entertainment."

— Lionel Fenn, author of *The Quest for the White Duck*

"The field needs more humorists of this calibre!"

— Robert Asprin

D1368955

Also by Craig Shaw Gardner

A Malady of Magicks
A Multitude of Monsters
A Night in the Netherhells
A Difficulty with Dwarves
An Excess of Enchantments

A Disagreement With Death

Craig Shaw Gardner

HEADLINE

Copyright © 1989 Craig Shaw Gardner

First published in Great Britain in 1989
HEADLINE BOOK PUBLISHING PLC

10 9 8 7 6 5 4 3

All rights reserved. No part of this publication may be
reproduced, stored in a retrieval system, or transmitted,
in any form or by any means without the prior written
permission of the publisher, nor be otherwise circulated
in any form of binding or cover other than that in which
it is published and without a similar condition being
imposed on the subsequent purchaser.

All characters in this publication are fictitious
and any resemblance to real persons, living or dead,
is purely coincidental.

ISBN 0 7472 3302 0

Printed and bound in Great Britain by
HarperCollins Manufacturing, Glasgow

HEADLINE BOOK PUBLISHING PLC
Headline House
79 Great Titchfield Street
London W1P 7FN

ACKNOWLEDGMENTS

Uh-oh. Here we are at the end of another trilogy. This time, I'd like to thank those people and things that made me The Way I am Today, specifically: Jay Ward and Bill Scott's *Rocky and Bullwinkle*, Walt Kelly's *Pogo*, Carl Bark's *Uncle Scrooge* and anything made by Chuck Jones; the writings of Robert Sheckley, Jack Sharkey and L. Sprague de Camp (often with Fletcher Pratt); Preston Sturges's movies; Stan Freberg commercials (who put those eight great tomatoes in that itty-bitty can?); Danny Kaye in Frank and Panama's *The Court Jester* (a partial prototype for Wuntvor—the vessel with the pestle holds the brew that is true); and almost anything made by those Monty Python people. In addition, much of these books was written while listening to the recordings of Louis Jordon ("Beware, Brother, Beware") and Kid Creole and the Coconuts ("Annie, I'm Not Your Daddy"). You have been warned.

The usual round of thanks must also go to my stalwart and long-suffering friends, including Jeff, Richard, Victoria and Mary (a.k.a. Team Cambridge), who critiqued this whole thing as it went along, and the lovely Elisabeth, who puts up with me wandering around the apartment chuckling at my own jokes. And then there's those New York people, like my Superagent, Merrilee Heifetz, and the entire friendly and helpful staff at Writers House; and also my Supereditor, Ginjer Buchanan, who almost always changes stuff back when I yell and scream, and everybody else at Berkley/Ace (Hi, Susan! Hi, Beth!).

Lastly, I would like to dedicate this, the last of the
Ebenezum books, to the memory of my grandfather
Walter W. Shaw
who introduced me to the world of art
and a world of wonders

ONE

There is one fact that every magician must accept: Sorcery is not a stable science. Quite the contrary, magic is ever-changing, and the nimble mage must learn to change with it. Magic is never done. It goes on forever and ever, constantly new, impossible to categorize or summarize. The magician must never consider a spell complete and successful until he or she sees the results. He must realize as well that every spell has a counterspell, and, in a world where magic rules, all things are possible. Using magic becomes a lifetime's work, as the mage discovers that all the spells and conjurations grow together into a force beyond the magician's simple goals, and further join with all the other spells, of all the other wizards, past, present and future, becoming an ever-changing tapestry beyond mortal ken, a force that no wizard can ever completely understand. Or completely take for granted.

That's magic in a nutshell. And that's my final word on the matter. I think.

—From *Spells That Hate Wizards,
and the Wizards Who Love Them*, third edition,
by Ebenezum, greatest wizard in the Western Kingdoms

"Wuntvor?"

I looked up. I realized that someone was calling my name, and perhaps had been doing so for quite some time.

"Wuntvor?" the young woman's voice repeated. It was the voice of my beloved, the witch Norei. "Do you want to talk?"

I shrugged. I did not care. After what had happened, I didn't care about much of anything. My master, Ebenezum, the greatest mage in the Western Kingdoms, was gone. He had been taken by Death. Worse still, Death had taken the wizard because the specter could not take me, whom it wanted because of some nonsense about my being the Eternal Apprentice, always instantaneously reborn into another apprenticing form, forever bumbling, forever helping heroes throughout eternity, and therefore forever beyond Death's grasp. And for this very reason—my supposed unobtainability by the creature to whom all came in time— Death desired me. The specter coveted my soul, and would go to any lengths to obtain it.

Norei squatted by my side, so that her face was even with mine. She gripped my chin with her cool, delicate fingers.

"Are you going to sit there for the rest of your life?"

When I did not reply immediately, she pulled her hand away. I blinked, glancing down at the dirt and grass between my knees, then looked up again at Norei's concerned expression. I sighed. I shrugged. Death had taken my master. What did it matter?

Norei whistled softly. "Alea was right."

"Alea?" I murmured. Had Alea been here?

Norei nodded, more to herself than to me. "When she told me that she had embraced you, and nestled her cheek tenderly next to your own, and promised you she would do anything, anything at all, to break you from this mood, and that, to all of this, you showed not the slightest reaction, I doubted her. Until now."

Alea had done what? I did not remember an embrace, and Alea was the sort of person, what with her long blond hair and trim actress's figure, with whom an embrace would be memorable. And there had been cheek nestling as well? And she had promised to do anything?

Anything? Well, not that I would have done *anything*, because, after all, I was promised to my beloved Norei. But still. Anything?

And I didn't remember any of it?

Norei frowned at me. "There must be some way we can get you out of this state."

I frowned back at her. I hoped that there was. Obviously, from what Norei had told me, the depression I was in was more serious than I had thought. I furrowed my brow, but the memory of Alea was lost to me.

Anything?

Norei reached out her arms to me and clasped me firmly.

"I think this calls for drastic action," she whispered, a grim half-smile upon her lips. She leaned in my direction.

What was she doing? My master was gone! I didn't have any time for such foolishness. Her full lips were much too close. I wanted to turn my head away.

For some reason, I did not.

I closed my eyes, and we kissed.

The kiss lasted for quite some time. I felt a tingling warmth in my chest, which spread outward as the kiss continued, until it heated me from the top of my head to the ends of my toes. And the true center of the warmth emanated from Norei's soft lips, the sweetest lips anyone had ever kissed.

The kiss ended at last. I gasped for breath. I opened my eyes.

Perhaps, I reconsidered, there was hope, after all.

"Now," my beloved said again. "Would you like to talk about it?"

I nodded, not yet able to speak.

"Ebenezum is gone," Norei summarized. "Death has taken him. But Death really wants you."

I nodded again. I marveled at my beloved. How could she be so clearheaded after such a kiss?

"And Death would be glad to trade your soul for Ebenezum's?"

I sighed. "I'm afraid so. That is, if we can trust Death. The specter is too fond of its games and tricks. I fear that, instead of releasing Ebenezum from its kingdom in exchange for me, Death may try to take us both."

"Humans!" an excruciatingly annoying voice exclaimed behind us. "Don't you know anything?"

I whirled to see the truth-telling demon Snarks, attired as usual in his monkish robes of somber gray; robes that, despite their neutral hue, still seemed to clash with the demon's bright green complexion.

I glared at the smirking Snarks.

"How long have you been here?" I demanded.

"Oh, long enough. Your kissing's not bad." The demon nodded pleasantly at Norei before turning back to me. "After we're alone, of course, I'll be glad to give you one or two pointers to improve your technique."

"Snarks!" I began, pointing back toward the clearing where the rest of our party rested. "If you don't—"

But my beloved put a restraining hand upon my elbow, stopping my tirade before it could properly begin. "No, no, let the demon be. I believe he has a point."

Snarks nodded his agreement. "Actually I have a number of them, but they're covered by my robes."

I was horrified. Norei and Snarks agreed about me? I could barely bring myself to look at my beloved as I asked: "You mean he's right about me having to improve my technique?"

Norei laughed softly. "No, no, your technique needs no improving whatsoever. Not to say that we both couldn't benefit from additional practice, whenever and wherever we can find the time." She kissed me gently on the cheek. "But I think he is correct when he implied that there might be more than one way to fight Death."

I didn't remember Snarks saying that. Still, after a prolonged bout of kissing, I had a tendency not to remember much of anything. What would my master have done in a case like this? After a moment's consideration, I nodded sagely and waited for one of the others to continue.

Snarks waved a sickly green finger at Norei. "The young witch is very perceptive, especially for a human.

When I came upon this cozy little scene, you were bemoaning the fact that Death seemed to control the situation. Typical limited human thinking.'' The demon paused to shrug his heavily robed shoulders. ''But then, you were not blessed with an upbringing spent in the devious byways of the Netherhells. One's thoughts flow much more freely when they're covered with a bit of slime.''

I listened intently to the small demon, for, although Snarks somehow always managed to phrase things in the most irritating manner imaginable, still much of what he had told us in the past had been of great use. The small demon had developed an odd clarity of vision, based in large part on his overwhelming compulsion to tell the truth in all things—a reaction, apparently, to an experience Snarks had while still in the womb, when his mother was badly frightened by a group of demonic politicians.

''So here we are,'' the demon continued, ''in the middle of a brand-new game, and Death appears to be holding all the cards.'' Snarks smiled. ''But I think that the game we're going to play won't use any cards at all. Who says we have to play by Death's rules? You have a crowd of allies only a few feet away, some of whom have very interesting powers. I think that, with a little thought, we will come up with a game that will actually put Death at a disadvantage.'' The demon clapped his hands enthusiastically. ''We can win this!''

''That's right!'' a tiny, high voice said from the vicinity of my ankles. ''You can't help but win with Brownie Power!''

Snarks paused mid-clap to make a face even more unpleasant than usual, as if something he had eaten recently was interfering with his digestion. He had also managed to turn an even deeper shade of green.

''Then again,'' he added a moment later, his stomach apparently once more under control, ''perhaps there are some of your allies who might be better excluded from further assistance.''

''Nonsense! Brownies need no rest. We thrive on conflict!'' Tap the Brownie performed an impromptu tap dance

as he spoke. "Especially if that conflict has something to
do with shoes!"

"I've got you there!" Snarks replied triumphantly. "I
don't think Death has anything at all to do with footwear!"

"Nonsense! A being of Death's stature, not wearing—"
Tap paused, doubt spreading across his tiny face. "Oh,
my. The specter's robes are rather long, aren't they?"

Snarks nodded triumphantly. "There's no way to tell if
Death wears shoes. There's no way to tell if Death even
has feet."

Oddly, the dismay seemed to vanish from the Brownie's
countenance, replaced by a faraway look in his eyes.
"Then Death may have spent millennia wandering the
cosmos shoeless?" Tap spoke in a voice barely above a
whisper. "Then—could it be—the first pair of shoes Death
wears might be made by me?"

"Indeed," I interjected, for the conversation seemed to
have wandered a good distance from our original topic.
"Perhaps, before we consider Death's footwear, we should
give a little more thought to the predicament of my
master—"

"Exactly what I was going to do." Snarks interrupted,
"before this shoe fanatic butted in."

"Shoe fanatic!" Tap blurted. "Well, if caring passion-
ately about one's footwear makes one a fanatic—if it
makes a difference to you about the proper heel size, and
the quality of the leather, and the aesthetic roundness of
the toe, and the elasticity of the laces, and the color of the
leather, using of course only true browns from nature, and
the correct eyelet placement, taking into account the proper
mathematical proportions, and the absolute best angle for
stitching the seams, and—well, ten or twelve other factors
equally important, then I guess you could call me—"

I tugged on Snarks's sleeve, drawing him a bit farther
away from the declaiming Brownie.

"My master," I repeated.

Norei walked up behind us. "We must find out what
Death has done with him. If the creature will tell us."

I smiled back at my beloved. Discussing my predicament with her and Snarks seemed to be restoring both my confidence and powers of thought.

"Why not?" I replied. "Death feels above us. I am sure we can get it to boast of my master's capture with no bother at all."

A green, scaly hand patted me briskly on the back. "Thinking worthy of the Netherhells!" Snarks exclaimed. "If you keep up this clever planning for—say—another three or four weeks, I may have to revise my opinion of humankind."

"But to make Death's shoes!" Tap shouted behind us. "I'd go down in the Brownie Hall of Fame! I can see the plaque now, made of that fine silver we use for our very best buckles: 'First footwear for Lord of the Dead, with heels designed to walk upon a billion souls. Designed by the humble—ME!' " Tap applauded his conjecture. "His Brownieship would have to forgive me then!"

Snarks looked back at the Brownie with some distaste. "Perhaps we should move even farther aside," he remarked, "say, to an entirely different clearing?"

I chided Snarks for his remark. After all, our tiny Brownie ally had been through a lot lately, what with his somewhat impetuous actions coming under criticism by his Brownie superiors, simply because he forgot he was supposed to wait for one of those superiors, and rushed to my aid instead. Now the head Brownie of them all, His Brownieship, was making noises about disbarring Tap from all future Brownie activity, which meant no more making shoes. In a situation like this, Tap was bound to be distraught. He deserved a little understanding.

Snarks nodded grimly when I was done. "Oh, I understand him all too well. But do I have to listen to him, too?"

The Brownie walked petulantly toward us. "You may scoff, but my whole future is at stake. I can't wait to meet Death and discuss footwear!"

In that instant, the sun disappeared behind a cloud. A wind sprang up from nowhere to remind us that summer was almost gone. And then the wind, too, was gone, replaced by a chuckle drier than a stone in a desert after a thirty-year drought.

"Somebody called?" the newcomer's voice rasped.

Tap began to tremble as he looked up at the newcomer's rotting robes. "On second thought, I might want a little more time to prepare for my discussion—" He paused as he backed hastily away. "Say, forty or fifty years?"

Death nodded at the Brownie. "Ah, yes. But we will talk, my little friend. Sooner or later."

The specter turned to me, the skull-like face beneath its hood showing all its teeth in a perpetual smile. "Ah, but there is no reason to be upset. This is naught but a courtesy call. As I recall, we have business to discuss. Something to do with an exchange of souls?"

I glanced at both Norei and Snarks, then stepped forward. I would have to handle this somehow. "Indeed." I tried to smile, but my lips would not refrain from trembling. "Do you have a proposal?"

Was it my imagination, or did Death's grin become even wider? "Oh, I have any number of them. But I don't think it's proper that proposals should come from me." Death's voice quickened, rising with every word. "After all, I am dealing with the Eternal Apprentice, the one being in the entire cosmos forever beyond my grasp!"

It stopped itself for a minute to smooth its dark, rotting robes. "At least, that is, until now," it added in a much more reasonable tone. "I therefore think it only proper that the initial proposal come not from me, but from the Eternal Apprentice."

"Indeed?" I replied. Death was taunting me, flaunting its advantage. Looking at the specter's smile, I felt the fear drain away, to be replaced by a building anger. If Death was going to play with me, I would play right back.

"You want a proposal, then?" I asked, managing a firm smile at last. "You give Ebenezum back to us and we would forget all about it."

Death made a strangled sound, deep in whatever it had that passed for a throat. "You dare—" it whispered. "When I could reach over and snuff out—" The specter paused again and stood up straight, regaining its skeletal composure. It laughed. "But I misunderstand. You wish to bargain. I apologize for my outburst, but I fear I am a bit too emotionally involved in these proceedings. I will go along with your game, of course. I am the master of games."

Death's knuckles clacked together noisily as it stroked its chin. "You have made an offer. It is, of course, unacceptable. However, I generously agree to make a counteroffer; say, let's forget all about the foolish wizard, and allow me rather to end this nonsense once and for all by taking you and your companions here to the Kingdom of Death for the rest of eternity."

Snarks sidled over to me. "I don't think this is working."

"Come, now," Death insisted. "I am waiting for your counteroffer."

"Indeed?" I answered, stalling for time. What could I bargain with next? I knew there was only one offer that would satisfy Death, and that was the possession of the Eternal Apprentice's soul. *My* soul.

Tap jumped across the clearing, landing on my shoe. "You'd better speak up. I don't think this guy is long on patience!"

"For once, we are in agreement," Snarks said, then added, "Why don't you offer the creature one of your companions in exchange for the wizard? Somebody with a useful skill, like making shoes."

"Then again," the Brownie reconsidered, "perhaps it is time to give this matter more thought. Perhaps fifty or sixty years more thought?"

"I await your answer," Death intoned. "Quickly, now! I have souls to collect!"

"Doom!" answered a deep voice behind me.

"Oh, here we go again," Death remarked fatalistically. "The longer we talk, the greater the number of companions to the Eternal Apprentice that will arrive. How many are there now? A dozen? Two dozen? May I suggest that we conclude our business before there are hundreds?"

"Indeed," I replied. "You will excuse me for a moment, but I need to consult with my fellows."

"Doom," the warrior Hendrek agreed as he walked forward to stand by my side.

"Of course," Death said with a sigh. "How could I expect anything else?"

Norei walked to stand by my other side. I motioned my companions to huddle together.

"What am I do to? Death demands a bargain. But what can we afford to bargain with?"

"We could offer the creature a sharp blow to the head," Hendrek suggested, hefting his cursed warclub, which no man could own but could only rent. It was the weapon called Headbasher, that stole the memories from men.

"A sharp blow to the head?" Norei frowned. "No, I don't think that was the sort of thing Wuntvor had in mind."

Hendrek nodded thoughtfully. "How about two sharp blows to the head?"

"You try my patience!" Death shrieked behind me. "You know what I desire. Make me an offer!"

"How about a little song and dance?" another voice boomed theatrically.

The earth shook as Damsel and Dragon bounded into the clearing. As serious as our situation was, I couldn't help glancing at Alea with her long blond hair and scanty vaudevillian attire.

Anything?

But I had no time for errant thoughts. Death was waving its bony arms in the air. It was becoming more agitated with every passing minute.

"We've come up with a special song for this occasion," Alea said brightly, tossing her long blond hair so that it shone even beneath the clouds.

Anything?

"Hit it, Hubert!" Alea called out.

"I will not allow this!" Death screamed. "I am here for negotiation, not vaudeville!"

But Damsel and Dragon had already started to shuffle back and forth. I knew a song could not be far behind.

Unfortunately, I was correct:

"There's something in the air that's pretty scary,
    The sun is gone, the wind's contrary!
    It's quite exciting, we must confeth;
    It must be time for a date with Death!"

"Say, Damsel," Hubert remarked. "Have you been introduced to Death?"

"Not officially," Alea replied jovially, "but I am dying to meet him!"

They launched into another verse:

"I must admit I'm feeling old,
    My youth is gone, the world is cold,
    All around me is such a meth,
    It must be time for a date with Death!"

"Say, Dragon," Alea interjected. "I've heard that Death is rather a cold character."

Hubert slapped a scaly knee before replying: "Well, Damsel, you've heard Dead Wrong!"

"No more!" Death pleaded. "Please, no more!" The specter turned to me. "Make me an offer, please!"

"Death wants an offer?" Hubert chortled triumphantly. "See, Damsel, I knew we could win him over! We simply have to face it. No one can resist our flashing feet and snappy patter!"

"No, no!" Death insisted. "I was speaking to the Eternal Apprentice!"

"Oh, trying to be hard-nosed about this, so we won't charge an arm and a leg?" Hubert laughed again. "You forget, Mr. Death, that we've had to face negotiators much worse than you. After all, we work in the arts!"

"But I guess he's seen right through us, Hubie," Alea added. "Let's face it, we need new worlds to conquer. We've already mastered the world above with our song and dance. And now we've almost finished this gig as official entertainment for Wuntvor's quest. Hubie and I have decided it's time to look for limited engagements elsewhere."

"Nothing fancy, mind you," Hubert continued. "One-night stands, mostly; perhaps a longer engagement in your population centers. If you have population centers." The dragon sighed happily. "Just think, the first song-and-dance act ever to tour the Kingdom of the Dead."

Death stared at me even more intently. "A bargain! Quickly!"

"I have an idea!" Snarks interjected. "You return the wizard to us, and we'll make sure the dragon and the woman never bother you again."

Death hesitated before it replied.

"Tempting," it said at last. "But not enough."

"Is this creature bothering you?" a magnificently modulated voice spoke close by my ear. I did not even have to turn my head to know that the unicorn had arrived.

"No, no, we were only talking."

The unicorn sighed. "Yes, I know; you will talk to creatures like this. But will you spare a few moments for me? It is enough to try even my perfect patience. Won't you ever find time for some"—the beast paused meaningfully—"'significant conversation?"

"It is time we got serious," Death interrupted hastily, as if afraid of being drowned out by the ever-increasing group of companions.

"So, you're having a party," yet another gruff voice commented loudly. "And you didn't wait for me?"

It was Jeffrey the wolf. "Hey. Never mind. I'm here now. It's amazing how a quest can come alive when there's a talking wolf along!"

"Or you will never see your master again!" Death shouted over the wolf.

"Doom," Hendrek added.

"Ho hey, ho hey! And after work we play!" a number of voices rang out in song. To my surprise, it was the Seven Other Dwarves.

"Hey!" the Brownie called. "You guys sing, too?"

"Do we sing, too?" one of the dwarves, whose name was Nasty, mimicked. "Of course we do, tiny. It's in our contract!"

"That is correct," sniffed another dwarve named Snooty.

"It is one of the privileges most cherished by the Dwarve Union. Not that you'd know anything about that!"

"Yes, yes, most certainly." Smarmy, the leader of the dwarves, stepped forward. "Singing happy work songs is a tradition greatly cherished by dwarvedom. Unfortunately, we are a bit out of practice, for Mother Duck never much liked it. But with her off fighting the Netherhells, we thought it was high time we got in a few verses."

"You guys ever think about going into vaudeville?" Hubert queried. "We're always looking for opening acts."

"Will someone listen to me?" Death demanded.

Norei clutched my hand. "Yes, Wuntvor," she said bravely. "We must come up with a bargain for Death."

"Bargains?" Death laughed bitterly, its patience at an end. "I am tired of bargains! You know what I desire!"

"Did I hear someone mention bargains?" A demon wearing a loud, checkered coat appeared before us, a large sack in one hand, a lit cigar in the other. He lifted the sack, waving it in Death's direction. "Well, you need look no further than my extensive stock of previously owned weapons!"

"No more!" Death screamed. "I will have my due! We will talk *now!*"

But suddenly another, much larger, much uglier demon stood among us. With a single, disdainful glance toward Death, the large demon cleared his throat and began to declaim:

"Guxx Unfufadoo, noble demon,
    Wishes to announce his presence—"

"Too much!" Death shrieked. "I will deal with all of you!" The creature lifted its hands above its head, spreading its bonelike fingers wide. And through the space between the fingers came the wind.

It began as a gale. Leaves were torn from the trees surrounding the clearing, then the smaller branches began to rip free. My companions tried to hold their ground, but they were forced to cover their faces so they would not choke on the dust that filled the air.

The wind increased, and the larger tree branches groaned as they bent in two. My smaller fellows lost their footing, and had to huddle on the ground so as not to be blown away. One by one, the others also fell to the ground as the enchanted gale redoubled again, becoming so powerful that even Hubert had to strain against its force.

Death smiled at me though the gale, as if we shared a joke. And perhaps we did, for I did not feel the wind at all.

"Good," Death remarked, its voice soft and clear despite the wind around us. "Now we may conclude our business."

"Indeed," I replied, and my voice, too, sounded louder than the wind. There would be no more stalling. I would have to make Death an offer at last. I looked at the huddled form of Norei to one side, the mass of overlarge robes that hid Snarks on the other side. There was no way I could talk to any of my fellows!

Death laughed, the sound of plants being ripped up by their roots in the gale. "They cannot help you now. My power has put us beyond them. It is just you and I: the Eternal Apprentice and his Death."

The specter wriggled his fingers. The wind grew even stronger.

"Their advice was worthless, anyway. Surprised that I should know?" Death paused an instant in its wind production to smooth its rotting robes. "You shouldn't be. I knew everything they've said, and everything they were going to say. Pitiful mortals. Do you think you can keep any secrets from Death? I am everywhere. I am in all of you, and make my presence known a little bit more every day. I know all of you intimately, and, although you may deny it, all of you know me, too."

Death laughed again, the sound of trees felled by lightning. "Now, though, you will come to know me so much better. For I have taken the two of us beyond the others. Prepare for your demise, Eternal Apprentice. No one can help you now.''

There was a crashing sound behind me. Perhaps the wind was actually tearing apart the trees. Death stared beyond me, as if astonished by its handiwork.

''Oops!''

A giant foot crashed between us, a foot that belonged to Richard the giant.

''Excuse me, fellows,'' Richard rumbled. ''There seem to be some tricky winds down close to the ground. It's making walking a little difficult. Uh— you didn't want that part of the forest back there, anyways, did you?''

''I don't believe this!'' Death screamed.

And then the wind was gone.

TWO

"Music hath charms to soothe the savage breast,"
or so the sages say. And I agree that, if you can hum
a little ditty or two, you will have nothing to fear from
the savage breast whatsoever. Unfortunately, 'tis an-
other matter entirely with savage fingers, savage claws,
savage teeth and savage fangs, all of which will
gladly shred and bite to their heart's content as you
provide the musical accompaniment.

—From *Wizardry in the Wild:*
A Sorceror's Guide to Outdoor Survival, fourth edition,
by Ebenezum, greatest wizard in the Western Kingdoms

Death had disappeared. But something was still wrong
with the forest.

My companions stood, one by one, in the aftermath of
the gale, each groaning, stretching, exclaiming or com-
plaining according to his or her nature. I looked around the
edges of the forest that bordered the clearing, to see if the
specter might be playing some trick on us. But I saw no
sign of its skeletal countenance. My large number of allies
had managed to overwhelm it once again. Death had had
to flee when faced by too much life.

Why didn't I feel happier about my victory? Was it

simply that my master was still a prisoner of Death, and our first meeting with the specter had been so chaotic that I had had no opportunity to discover any further hint of Ebenezum's whereabouts? Or was there something more? Had there been a change in the forest, beyond the fact that it was a mass of splintered trees and squashed bushes where the giant passed through?

"Oops," Richard interrupted. "Could someone tell me what is going on?"

"Doom," Hendrek answered.

"Do you think this means Death isn't interested in new entertainment attractions for his kingdom?" Hubert wondered.

I asked my companions to calm down for a moment. There was something out beyond the clearing. If I listened for it, perhaps I could discover what it was.

After a muttered comment or two, my allies quieted. I stared out over the demolished corner of the forest, and listened. Perhaps, I realized, the wind had not vanished entirely. Though far less violent than before, it was still out there, blowing about the splintered wood, whispering through the uprooted leaves.

Whispering? As soon as the thought entered my head, I realized how apt an analogy I had found. For the wind did not blow mindlessly through the newly dead wood beyond the clearing. Rather, there was a pattern to the ebb and flow of the breeze, as if it blew against the leaves and branches to make specific sounds; words perhaps, phrases, even parts of sentences. I strained to hear what the wind was saying.

". . . not . . ." said the breeze through the branches. And then: ". . . not gone . . ."

"Doom," Hendrek murmured, but I waved him to silence.

"I am not . . ." the breeze whispered. "I am still . . . your answer . . . waiting for your answer."

"Death!" I whispered in reply. For I was sure it was the specter, speaking to me through the broken trees.

". . . cannot escape . . . everywhere . . . Death is . . ."

This was too strange. I had to investigate, even though

it was surely one of Death's tricks. But I knew I would have to face Death's tricks and more if I was to rescue my master. I stepped forward and drew my sword.

"What do you want *now?*" Cuthbert, my enchanted blade, yelped. "There isn't going to be blood, is there?"

I looked out at the dead forest. Now that I had walked closer to the ruined wood, I noticed that the forest floor was covered by wisps of fog that seemed to be moving in anything but a random pattern, as if they were following some predetermined design.

"No," I answered quite honestly. "I don't believe there will be blood."

"Oh, no," Cuthbert moaned. "I know what that tone of voice means. There might not be any blood, but there's going to be plenty of ichor!"

I nodded grimly, for I could make no other answer. The sword was probably right. Any moment now, there would be ichor and more.

"Oops?" Richard called from where he stood, high above us all. "Pardon me, but is there something going on down there? It's so difficult to see anything clearly from my vantage point."

"Indeed," I replied. "It is difficult for us to see as well. We will have to investigate."

"Doom."

I glanced to my side, and saw Hendrek pacing me, step for step, his cursed warclub, Headbasher, swinging in his very large hand.

"Hendrek's right, even if he does refuse to lose weight," the annoyingly correct voice of Snarks came from my other side. His scaly green hands held a stout oak staff. "If we're going to fight this, we have to fight together."

"Don't you think it would be a good idea if you took someone with a knowledge of spells along?" Norei called as she caught up to the rest of us.

I gave my beloved a welcoming smile, then looked forward again into the dead forest. The fog was thickening as it lifted from the ground, a whorling gray mass that rose and fell violently, as if it were a great, gray blanket hiding an army of fiends beneath.

There was a small explosion by my feet. It was Tap the Brownie. He pointed at the roiling fog.

"Pretty creepy, huh? This looks like a job for Brownie Power!"

I stood still for a moment while the little fellow hopped into my pocket.

"Begin!" a huge voice spoke behind me.

Brax the salesdemon began to beat out a regular rhythm on a small drum he carried with him for this very purpose, while his fellow demon, Guxx Unfufadoo, declaimed:

> "Guxx Unfufadoo, soldier demon,
>   Marches bravely into battle,
>   With no thought of his own peril,
>   Does it all for his friend Wuntvor!"

There was a moment's silence, followed by Guxx Unfufadoo's curt demand:

"Ask me!"

"Hmm?" Brax replied. "Oh, sorry, I forgot, I was putting away my dru—"

"The question!" Guxx insisted.

"Oh, yes!" Brax groveled. "Most certainly, Grand Hoohah." I heard the rustle of parchment. Brax cleared his throat. "Tell me, Guxx," he read in a monotone. "Why are you making this noble sacrifice?"

"Sacrifice? I see." Guxx paused a moment to consider, then commanded:

"Resume!"

Brax resumed beating the drum.

> "Guxx Unfufadoo, abused demon,
>   Wrongly thrown from power below us;
>   Knows if he helps lad in trouble,
>   Wuntvor will return the favor!"

Return the favor? Did that mean Guxx expected me to go back down to the Netherhells with him and help him regain his power? Was that why he was aiding me? Perhaps, I thought, in all fairness, I should let the large

demon know that another visit to the slime pools below
was not in my immediate plans.

"Indeed—" I began

"Wait a minute, Damsel!" Hubert yelled enthusiastically.
"Guxx's declaiming puts me in the mood for a little song!"

Our march had brought us almost to the edge of the
ruined wood, and I could see the first fingers of fog
perhaps two dozen paces ahead. Some of them curled
together as we approached, as if beckoning us to hurry. It
was no longer the time for song, or declamation.

"Ind—" I tried to interject.

"Continue!" Guxx roared over my objection.

> "Guxx Unfufadoo, angered demon,
>   Does not speak for entertainment,
>   Lifts his voice for but one purpose,
>   To put some fear in those he fights with!"

"Indeed—" I began again, but my heart was no longer
in the conversation. I could not risk turning around while
the wisps of fog gathered about me.

"No need to thank us!" Hubert assured me. "If simple
declamation can keep Death's minions at bay, think what
we might accomplish with a little song and dance."

"That's right, Dragon," Alea echoed Hubert's enthusiasm, "especially if we come up with something appropriate. Say, 612?"

"A wonderful choice!" Hubert agreed. "Shall we?"

The two of them sang together:

> "It's getting scary out here in the big, wide world,
>   With creatures that jump and go boo!
>   But no matter what horrible monster we meet,
>   I'm not at all scared about you."

"Recommence!" Guxx screamed forcefully. Brax beat
the drum more quickly.

> "Guxx Unfufadoo, music critic,
>   Has had enough of this pair's singing!

Is ready to perform a service;
Perhaps some vocal cords need pruning?''

The demon flexed his claws meaningfully as he blew his nose. I realized he had come very close to making a true rhyme.

"Well, you know how we feel about that!" Hubert replied. "Take it, Damsel!"

Alea took it:

"It's so frightening that we want to hide,
For whatever else can we do?
Something really nasty—"

They both paused to point at Guxx.

"—might be by our side!
But I'm not at all scared about you!"

Guxx Unfufadoo began to jump up and down, his clawed fists punching invisible enemies before him, a fearsome grimace spread upon his countenance. All in all, the demon seemed even more angry than usual.

"Override!" he shrieked.

Brax drummed even more loudly than before.

"Doom." Hendrek, oblivious to the drama taking place between our more theatrical companions, used Headbasher to point into the shattered forest before us.

Oddly enough, the fog did seem to be retreating. Could whatever was waiting for us out there be a music critic as well? Perhaps the fog just didn't care for noise. Whichever the reason, the forest floor before us was fog-free for a hundred paces.

"This could be a trap," Hendrek grumbled.

"And I could have relatives living in the Netherhells," Snarks added. "You have an amazing talent, dear Hendrek, for stating the obvious."

Hendrek solemnly nodded in agreement. "It is a gift."

The drumming redoubled behind us, twice as loud. I

was amazed that so much noise could come from one tiny
drum. Once agin, the demon declaimed behind us:

> "Guxx Unfufadoo, angered demon,
> Has had enough of caterwauling!
> Seems you should have used your heads which
> From your necks will soon be falli—"

The demon's declamation dissolved in a fearsome bout
of sneezing.

"Such a waste," Brax sighed behind us. "What a
magnificent rhyming talent!"

Even I had to admit, it was a pity. Guxx Unfufadoo, the
dread rhyming demon, had been defeated by a counterspell
performed by my master which caused the creature, once
strengthened by his rhymes, to sneeze violently whenever
rhymed poetry was present in his speech. Now—even
though Guxx had once been our sworn enemy—still I
found it sad to see him reduced to a mere sneezing shadow
of his former demonic nastiness.

"What's this?" Hubert exclaimed. "Guxx has given
up?"

" 'Tis a pity," Alea agreed. "You might say he's lost
by a nose."

"Gee, Damsel!" the dragon enthused. "That sounds
like a cue for another verse!"

"Oops!" a voice rumbled from above. "No, it doesn't."

"It doesn't?" Damsel and Dragon asked in unison.

The ground shook behind me, the sound, I guessed, of
Richard putting his foot down.

"It doesn't," the giant repeated. "There is something
strange going on out there."

"Oh," Hubert replied meekly, "I guess it doesn't. Oh,
well. The rest of the verses weren't all that good, anyway.
In fact, the seventh and fifteenth stanzas were a trifle
redundant—" The dragon's voice trailed off. "Something
strange?"

Snarks laughed. "I never knew it could be so useful to
have a giant along." But then he turned to look out at the
dead wood before us. "Oh" was his only comment.

"Doom." Hendrek pointed again with his club. In the sudden silence, the fog had begun to creep back across the debris-strewn ground. "Whatever is out there is coming back for us."

"Indeed," I replied, doubt creeping into my voice. Should I encourage the vaudevillian duo's singing, after all? It was, at best, a difficult decision. Aloud, I mused: "What sort of trap advances on its prey?"

"Ah," a magnificently modulated voice spoke immediately behind me, "but whatever is out there will realize soon that *it* is what has been trapped, once it has been pierced by my glorious golden horn."

"Hey!" Jeffrey added from somewhere nearby. "And don't they know that no trap is complete unless you have a talking wolf along?"

I realized the Seven Other Dwarves were with us as well, as I heard them singing quietly in the background:

"Ho hee, ho hee,
     No trap will bother we!"

I wished I had the dwarves' confidence. Couldn't they see what was happening? The fog's turbulence was increasing with every second it roiled toward us. And as it grew closer, I could see that it was not all a uniform gray, but actually showed spots of dully gleaming color here and there that swam within the mist. And the colors grew in intensity here, and faded there, like the flicker of sickly strings of lights, as if whatever was hiding within the mist was rising to the surface.

The voices within the fog were louder, too. For I realized that there was more than one calling out to me. Now that there was no more singing or declaiming, I could hear them much more clearly:

"Wuntvor—"

"—business is not finished—"

"Eternal Apprentice—"

"—come to us, Wuntvor—"

"—over so quickly—"

"Why don't you put down your sword?"

"—an end to eternity—"

"Wuntvor—"

"Let us caress you—"

"We will cover you so comfortably—"

"—over so quickly—"

"Wouldn't you like to rest—forever?"

"You heard what they said?" Cuthbert wailed. "About putting down your sword?"

"Indeed," I answered.

"Isn't that a good idea?" the sword pleaded hopefully. "Letting me rest someplace dry, say back behind us, away from the fog?"

I grunted in reply. "The way this fog moves, I have the feeling there is no place it could not cover, and no way we might escape it. I suppose I might give you a choice: Would you like to be stuck flat upon the ground, inanimate, while the clammy fog encloses you? Or would you like to be held in my hands, fighting your way to freedom?"

"That's a choice?" The sword shivered, and spoke in a resigned tone: "Very well. Ichor is my destiny."

"Indeed," I replied, and advanced upon the fog.

THREE

"Don't quote me. No comment."

—Statement of Ebenezum,
greatest wizard in the Western Kingdoms,
when first approached about Wizardgate

"Wuntvor—" the fog called out to me. Or perhaps it was something hiding in the fog. Or any number of things hiding in the fog.

"—come to us, Wuntvor—"

I looked to my companions. We were all together, a tight-knit group.

"—bring your friends—"

Hendrek and Snarks flanked me on either side, their weapons drawn. They were moving more cautiously than before. We had slowed our headlong rush to meet our destiny. The surrounding mist was far too strange. None of us could guess what might emerge from the dense grayness at any instant, and we all realized that we had to adjust our moves accordingly.

"We've been waiting—" the fog voices whispered.

"Doom," Hendrek said, his voice softer than before, as if the fog that reached to encircle us was a greater threat than even his pessimism could comprehend.

The fog voices answered in a jumble:

"—Eternal Apprentice—"

"—ever so long—"

"We are so comforting—"

"—Wuntvor—"

"This is all a little depressing," Snarks remarked with a lot less venom than usual.

This situation, apparently, was affecting all of us. I looked about. Norei was right behind me, flanked by the unicorn and the talking wolf. Guxx and Brax were next, the salesdemon grasping his drum, ready to beat at a moment's notice. The Seven Other Dwarves followed them, while Hubert took up the rear with Alea perched upon his scaly blueish-purple neck.

We had been quite spread out when we had begun our march toward the fog, but now the rear guard seemed to be catching up with the front ranks, so that we were all in a bunch, threatening to trod on each other's feet at a moment's notice. Perhaps it was that those of us in front had been slowing our pace. Or perhaps those in the rear had quickened theirs to keep away from the tendrils of mist that curled about their heels.

"—Wuntvor—"

I took an even smaller step toward the fog. What did the mist want from me?

"—that's the way—"

"—almost—"

"—only a moment—"

"—over so peacefully—"

Indeed, I thought. But for some reason, I could not bring myself to say even that single word. In fact, I couldn't bring myself to do much of anything. Somehow, my steps had slowed so much that I had trouble pushing my foot forward to take another. What was wrong here?

I turned to ask my companions. They had all stopped walking as well. In fact, they seemed to have stopped moving entirely. All of them stared forward, into the fog. Hubert blinked, slowly. I looked down into the pocket of my jerkin. The Brownie appeared wedged inside, hands covering his tiny cap, as if he never wanted to look up into the light of day again.

"Doo—" Hendrek began, but was unable to finish the word.

Something awful was happening!

"—Wuntvor—" The fog called my name instead.

"—over so quickly—"

"—and ever so final."

The Seven Other Dwarves sang listlessly:

"Hi hor, hi hor,
  Why bother anymore?"

Then all eight of them began to snore.

Indeed, I thought. Why bother? The fog encircled us. In a matter of minutes, it would cover us as well. It was easier this way. No bother at all.

Norei forced her eyes open, as if she had to fight from falling asleep as well. "Oh, no!" she gasped, stifling a yawn. "Can't you see, Wunt—" Her eyes closed, and she slept.

"Norei?" I managed, but could not muster my thoughts sufficiently to frame a further question. And yet my beloved was trying to tell me something. I watched the tendrils of mist encircle her ankles.

The fog! It was the fog that was doing this! That's what Norei had tried to tell me. This gray mass about us was more than a physical presence. It affected our emotions as well, draining our will to resist.

Well, it wouldn't work on me! Why bother? I had asked myself a moment before while under the influence of the dreadful mist. I had to bother, no matter what the fog told me. My master's life depended on it! And the lives of my companions as well! Death would have to try harder still to defeat Wuntvor, the Eternal Apprentice. Not even something as insidious as a cursed fog could defeat me!

Or could it?

I blinked; a movement that took all my concentration. I knew what was troubling us at last, but I also knew I had no energy left to defeat it. I had used up all my reserves in one last burst of defiant thought, leaving me filled with the lethargy of death. And it looked like my other companions, Norei included, were in a worse state still. All of them, Brownie, unicorn, dragon, wolf, dwarves, demons and maiden—all of them were lost in deadly sleep.

My eyelids were too heavy. I felt them close, and my chin loll forward against my chest. But it couldn't end like this! Somewhere, deep within me, defiance still lived. Somehow, I had to reach it, to coax it to the surface, to fill me with its power and give me strength. I could feel it now, like a hot coal burning deep within my brain. I had to use that coal to set fire to my mind, and find some way to overcome the mist that surrounded us.

My eyes fluttered open for an instant. Using every shred of defiance I had left in me, I only had the strength for one more word:

"Help!"

"Oops!" came a reply from on high. And then there came a wind. Death's wind, I thought, as I drifted toward sleep. This time, even the giant would not escape the grip of Death.

"Wait—" the fog whispered.

"—fair at all—"

"—heard the last—"

"—stupid giant—"

Then the voices were lost to the ever-increasing gale.

The wind stopped a moment later, and my eyes fluttered open.

The fog was gone. We were surrounded by brilliant sunlight.

"Oops," Richard called. "Did I blow too hard?"

My companions let out a ragged cheer. Apparently, they were every bit as awake as I.

"Not at all!" I shouted aloft. "You have saved us from a dire fate!"

"Doom," Hendrek agreed.

"Gone?" my sword cried in disbelief. "It's gone?"

"But it wasn't me at all," Richard replied. "I was acting on your direction."

"I don't have to *do* anything?" the sword rejoined. "I don't have to *cut* anyone?" There seemed to be an edge of hysteria in its voice.

"Nonsense, big fellow!" Jeffrey objected to the giant's humility. "It was a wonderful rescue. Even a talking wolf couldn't have done any better!"

"No blood?" Cuthbert shrilled. "No ichor? No slicing? No dici—" I slid the sword back into its scabbard. It obviously needed a rest.

The large fellow blushed, his face as crimson as the setting sun. "Well, gee," he murmured. "It's so difficult to see what's going on down there. There was all this fog, and nobody seemed to be doing much of anything. And then the apprentice yelled. What was I to do? I simply felt it was time to make a giant effort."

"He's good on his rescues," Snarks remarked. "His speeches could use work."

"Oops," Richard responded. "But that's one of my problems. Being a giant is a lonely job." He sighed. "Think of it. Whenever you hear one of my kind mentioned, it's almost always in the singular. You know, 'There's a giant tearing up such-and-such a place!' or 'A giant's laying waste to so-and-so's domain!' My kind doesn't like to get together in bunches. A crowd of giants is even too big for us! You know, it's a wonder my father and mother met at all. Lucky for me, they were terrorizing neighboring kingdoms. Otherwise, I never would have been born!"

"Indeed," I replied, trying to think of a nice way to quiet the giant down. Not that I wasn't grateful for our rescue by the big fellow; in fact, I planned to thank him all over again once we had reached safer territory.

Right now, however, we were anything but safe, for I was sure Death still lurked about. We had driven the specter away in its skeletal state, and we had blown away its killer fog. But I had no reason to believe that we had seen the last of it.

"And another thing," Richard continued. "It's hard to get close to people. Let's face it, I could crush any of you without even thinking!"

"Doom," Hendrek murmured close to my ear. "I think I should take a look around."

Richard sighed more deeply still. The few trees left in

the vicinity bent under the weight of the breeze. "Being a giant isn't easy. There's not a lot of us around. It's very difficult to socialize."

"Good idea," I replied to the large warrior. "I fear Death is near us still. Take some of the others with you."

Hendrek left my side, motioning for Jeffrey, Snarks and Norei to accompany him.

"I suppose that's why I fell in with Mother Duck," the giant went on. "She was very good at giving orders. And I found myself very comfortable taking them."

Hendrek strode forward into the dead forest, the other three forming a tight-knit group behind him. They were a formidable unit. Between Hendrek's club, Jeffrey's teeth and claws, Norei's spells and Snarks's sharp tongue, they should be able to defeat almost anything thrown against them.

"Still, I found myself increasingly disturbed over Mother Duck's need to control everybody," the giant went on, "especially after she got hold of all of you. It took my heart out of gianting." Richard sighed even more prodigiously. Small branches ripped free of nearby tree trunks.

"Methinks," he added, " 'tis time to go into another line of work."

There was a moment's silence. Richard was done at last.

"Have you considered vaudeville?" Hubert suggested.

"Doom!" The intensity of Hendrek's statement cut short Richard's answer. We all turned to see what had upset the warrior so.

Hendrek pointed with his warclub at the forest floor.

"The branches," he intoned, "They are moving of their own accord."

Now that the warrior mentioned it, I did think I saw pieces of dead wood twisting like snakes through the debris.

"Will they attack us?" Jeffrey whispered.

"Not unless they plan to attack us with words," Snarks replied. "They're forming themselves into letters."

"Stay close!" Norei warned. "This could be a trick."

"The perceptiveness of you humans never ceases to astound me," Snarks commented.

"Doom! They are forming words!"

"Oh, yeah!" Jeffrey frowned as he read, "Sur-ren-der, Wuntvo—" He looked up at the others. "That's all it says, so far."

"Watch out!" Norei yelled.

The animate branches must have finished their spelling, for they rose quickly into the air, heading straight for my four companions.

"Back, foul wood!" Hendrek exclaimed, lifting his club behind his head.

"Urk!" Jeffrey the wolf, who had been standing too close behind the large warrior, replied. Headbasher had done its hellish work again.

But Norei was busy as well. She made three quick passes in the air. The flying branches fell to the ground.

"There!" she said with some satisfaction. "Death will have to do better than that!"

"Who?" Jeffrey queried. "What?" The wolf's voice shifted down a register.

"Indeed," he said rather more calmly. "Wuntvor, listen quickly."

I would recognize that voice anywhere.

"Master!" I cried.

"Indeed," the wolf replied. "Death is distracted for the moment by your resourcefulness. But we must make plans for my escape. Death is keeping me prisoner in his king—"

Jeffrey's mouth snapped shut, but opened a moment later.

"Indeed?" a much drier voice remarked, the sound of sand wearing grooves into granite. "What a clever wizard your Ebenezum is, contacting you behind my back. But no one is cleverer than Death." The specter laughed, the sound of fish drowning in the open air. The wolf stared with hate-filled eyes, and silence surrounded us, as if all the world was waiting for the words of death.

The wolf looked away from us. "I have had enough nonsense! I think it is time I made my final offer. Listen carefully, if you ever expect to see your wizard again!"

FOUR

*The sages say that "running is good for the health,"
and, for once, I agree with the sages, especially in
those cases when one is being chased by anything
carrying weapons, claws, legal summons, fire-breathing
capability or any combination of the above."*

—From *The Teachings of Ebenezum*,
Volume XXXIV.

"Ebenezum is dead," the wolf said with the specter's
voice, "unless you intervene." Jeffrey paused to grin.
"No, no. 'Intervene' is not the proper word. The correct
word is 'sacrifice.' "

"Indeed?" I responded, my voice strong despite the
queasy feeling that threatened to rise from my stomach.
Death wanted to talk again. This time I would have to get
the information I wanted.

"I should take you now!" the wolf growled. "But no.
Coming to me has to be your decision, made with your
own free will. Oh, how the fates conspire against me!
Otherwise you will continue to be the Eternal Apprentice"
—the wolf shuddered—"forever. But, should you choose
thusly"—Jeffrey allowed himself a deadly smile—"your
master will remain with me, forever. Yes, you heard what

32

the clever wizard said. I have already taken him to the Kingdom of the Dead, and the only way he will ever leave is if you replace him.''

"Indeed," I commented again, doing my best to think fast. "Then you wish me to come with you now, with no argument, no elaboration, nothing whatsoever?"

"Well, yes," the wolf replied, the slightest doubt entering his spectral voice, "that's the general idea. Otherwise, you know, your master—"

"Yes, yes, I know all about my master," I interrupted hastily. "But it does seem rather dull and boring, unimaginative even, for you to simply whisk me away from the land of the living."

"Dull? Boring? Unimaginative?" Jeffrey gnashed his teeth. "Death is anything but that! I know more interesting ways to die than—"

"I'm certain you do," I interjected again. "And I'll be glad to try any of them that you like."

"You will?" The wolf's mouth opened in surprise. "Any of them?"

"Certainly," I replied. "You can try three or four of them in a row on me if you like."

"You mean I can kill the Eternal Apprentice three or four times in a row?" Jeffrey clapped his forepaws. "You're too good to me. When can we start?"

"Not quite yet," I answered. "I think we have time to play a little game first."

"Game?" The wolf paused, scowling at me. "I am the master of games!"

"Indeed." I allowed myself the slightest of smiles. This was working better than I had hoped. "Then you will not object to playing one with someone as unskilled in gamesmanship as myself. Of course, to keep the game interesting, there will have to be a prize for the winner."

"A prize?" the Death-wolf retorted vitriolically. "Like the time I arm-wrestled your master, and he tricked me out of an entire kingdom? You must think Death a fool! I will not be swindled like that again!"

"Indeed? Well, if that's the way you feel about it"—I

paused to yawn—"I suppose we have nothing else to talk about."

"But you'll never see your master again!" Death declared.

"My master?" I replied quizzically, as if I could barely be bothered to make conversation. "Oh, yes, the wizard. 'Tis a pity if he has to die, but let's be realistic. He was rather old already, wasn't he? How many years would he have left, even if you didn't take him now?"

"But—" Death was so astonished that it took the creature a moment to collect its spectral thoughts. Finally, the wolf blurted: "You must save your master!"

"Must I?" I blew casually upon my knuckles. "I don't see why. Without a game, it hardly seems worth it."

"Without a game?" The wolf took a deep breath, then laughed, the sound of small plants shriveling beneath a winter's frost. "Why am I worried? I am the master of games; you have said so yourself. I was defeated once, but it was by your master, a wily old wizard. You are naught but a young and awkward apprentice, even if you are eternal." Jeffrey once again allowed himself a smile. "Besides, you have made promises to me. You, the Eternal Apprentice. You *will* die three or four times?"

"If I lose the game?" I shrugged. "I suppose I will have to."

Death's laughter redoubled. "You will experience half a dozen deaths before I am through, each one more lingering and unpleasant than the one before! That is our bargain!"

"Indeed?" I replied, still appearing only mildly interested. "I suppose it might be, if—when I win—you return my master to the land of the living unharmed, and take no one else in his stead."

"Oh, I might as well." Death chuckled. "Half a dozen deaths!" Jeffrey's eyes stared into my own.

"So what is the game?" he demanded.

"Indeed," I replied. This was all going a bit too well. And more than a little too quickly. I allowed myself a world-weary sigh before I spoke again. "Why do we have to rush these matters so? We have just struck the bargain. You must give me some little time to think, so that I might come up with something worthy of your talents."

"Really?" Death paused for a moment to consider my request. "Well, I suppose there is no harm in allowing you to reflect on your impossible situation for a little while longer. Besides, it will give me a few more hours to gloat. Half a dozen deaths! And they will be quite imaginative deaths, I assure you. Very well. I shall return at midnight." The wolf winked broadly at me and my assembled companions. "It's the time of day that suits me best, don't you think?"

Death laughed again as we were surrounded by a moment of intense wind. And then the gale was gone, as quickly as it had arrived.

Jeffrey blinked. "Hey!" he yelled at Hendrek. "You should watch where you throw that warclub." The wolf rubbed the hirsute lump atop his head. "Why is everybody staring at me?"

"Doom," the warrior replied. "You were the vessel for Death."

Jeffrey took a step away. "That doesn't mean you're going to hit me again, does it? Can't you take a little constructive criticism?"

"No, he can't," Snarks replied for the warrior, "though Netherhells knows I've tried."

"But Hendrek isn't going to attack you again," I interjected. "He was trying to tell you that when his dread warclub robbed you of your memory, Death stepped in to speak through your temporarily vacated brain, using your mouth and body to give us his ultimatum!"

"Really? Death spoke through me?" The wolf rolled his tongue over his very large incisors. "So that's why my mouth tastes like rotting leaves." Jeffrey wrinkled his snout. "Fauugghh! Maybe I should eat something else to clear the pallet. How long has it been since I've had a square meal, anyway? And to think I came to Mother Duck's kingdom because it had a reputation for fine cuisine."

"Fine cuisine?" Norei replied with some trepidation.

"Doom," Hendrek added.

"Delicacies," Jeffrey explained. "You know, pigs, small

girls dressed in red, grandmothers. The talking wolf's diet is surprisingly varied.''

Snarks waved at Jeffrey with his staff. "Well, why don't you be a good talking wolf and go out looking for them? I'm sure there's a grandmother out there somewhere. In the meantime, we have to make plans.''

"Doom," Hendrek agreed.

"Your friends are right," Norei remarked forcefully. "We must plan quickly, but we are only able to plan through your efforts, Wuntvor. You were magnificent, in the way you handled Death."

Norei took my hand as she spoke, and I could not help but smile when I heard such a compliment from my beloved. Still, as flattering as Norei's words were, I felt that I did not truly deserve them. Instead, I told my companions I owed it all to my master. I had thought about how Ebenezum had dealt with Death when we had first met the specter, then done nothing more than follow the wizard's example.

"You are too modest—" Norei began.

"That's almost as good as Brownie Power!" Tap added.

"I always knew he had greatness in him," the unicorn interjected. "What an apprentice! What a lap!"

The dwarves cheered as one:

"Ho hi, ho hi,
  He's our kind of guy!"

"So what is your plan?" Snarks interrupted.

I told them I didn't have one.

"Doom," Hendrek remarked.

I explained that my experience with the wizard only went so far. Ebenezum had taught me how to find Death's weaknesses. However, now that I had found them, I wasn't too sure what to do with them. My master had used a combination of arm wrestling and sneezing to defeat the specter before. But Death would be ready for similar tricks. If I wanted to defeat Death and regain my master, I would have to devise something entirely new.

"So you have absolutely no plan whatsoever?" Snarks clarified.

"Indeed," I replied.

"Doom," Hendrek chorused.

The Seven Other Dwarves stepped forward.

"Hi haid, hi haid,
Wuntvor needs our aid!"

Smarmy took an extra step forward. He held forth a large glass sphere.

"Beg pardon," the self-effacing dwarve remarked. "But, worthless though we may be, we thought we might be able to make some small, pitiful contribution to the continuation of your noble quest. In that spirit, we have made some efforts, minuscule though they may be, to procure something that, even in some insubstantial way, you might use to—"

"Shut up and give him the thing!" Nasty called.

"Oh, my," Smarmy replied. "Oh, yes."

I took the glass globe from his outstretched hands.

"It's a crystal ball," Norei said, a bit of wonder in her voice. "Isn't it?"

"Oh, my," Smarmy answered. "Oh—yes, it is. Not much of a crystal ball, perhaps, but it was the best we poor, insignificant—"

"It looks like a very nice crystal ball to me," Norei interrupted. "Doesn't it, Wuntvor?"

"Indeed," I answered. "I am quite flattered. Wherever—"

"We stole it from Mother Duck!" Nasty brayed. "She has tons of this stuff. Claims she needs it for her fairy stories!"

"I hope it's all right." Smarmy sighed. "It was so hard finding something appropriate. You already had an enchanted weapon and any number of magical companions. I mean, what do you give to the apprentice who has everything?"

"Indeed," I replied heartily. "How does it work?"

Smarmy hit his forehead with both of his wringing

hands. "Oh! How forgetful can I be? There's a rhyme that goes with it!" He pulled a crumpled piece of parchment from his pocket and handed it to me.

"The Incantation," the parchment read. "Be sure to state quickly and in a loud voice:

"Secret sphere, seashore seer,
    Surely showing sunshine seeking.
    Simply said, the shaft is shed,
    Spouting spells that send us shrieking!"

"It should be clear enough," Smarmy prompted. "Just recite the incantation, and the crystal will show you whatever you wish. What could be simpler? And once you get the hang of it, it will show you anything, or anyone, you want."

"Indeed?" I asked, genuinely intrigued. "Including my master?"

"Oops!" the giant interrupted from on high.

All conversation ceased down below. Considering what had transpired before, when Richard said "Oops," we listened.

"What is the matter?" I called aloft.

The giant scraped a foot along the ground. The one tree still standing in his vicinity was reduced to splinters.

"I would like to ask a boon," Richard said meekly.

"Indeed," I answered. 'If it is in my power, you shall have it."

The giant smiled. "Good. What should I do next?"

"Beg pardon?" I asked, for I did not quite understand his request.

"Well, that is, you see, I told you about Mother Duck's need to control everything? Including me?"

"Indeed?"

Richard shook his head unhappily. "I got used to it. Without her to boss me around, I'm not quite sure what to do."

The Seven Other Dwarves nodded sympathetically.

"We know exactly what the giant's talking about!" Smarmy exclaimed. "Now that Mother Duck is gone, we have all the freedom we want. But what do we want to do with it?''

"Oh, wow," Spacey ventured.

"We could travel," Sickly coughed. "I wouldn't mind a better climate."

"Move somewhere that had a better class of creatures," Snooty mentioned.

"Sneak up behind people and scream," Noisy suggested.

"How about finding new and interesting things to drop?" Clumsy asked.

"You see?" Smarmy interjected. "It's so difficult to find a consensus!"

"Oops," Richard agreed. "But you haven't answered my question. What am I supposed to do? What is my function in the story? I need direction. I need motivation."

"Indeed," I murmured. "That's a big problem."

"Exactly," the giant stated. "Free will can be frightening."

"Might I again suggest vaudeville?" Hubert interjected helpfully. "There's very little free will involved."

"But there is a lot of dancing," Alea said.

"Dancing?" The giant looked doubtfully down to his feet.

"And snappy patter!" Hubert quickly added.

"Snappy patter?" Richard sounded interested. "That might be nice. Life gets tedious when all you can ever say is 'Time for Mother Duck's ovens.' A constant diet of threats is so limiting."

It seemed to me that I should add something to this conversation as well. It also seemed to me that there had to be other options beyond vaudeville.

"Indeed—" I began, but was distracted by a high-pitched sound that was rapidly approaching.

"Eep eep!" a tiny voice cried. "Eep eep!"

I would recognize those eeps anywhere. It was my magic ferret, back from doing whatever magic ferrets do.

"I think he's trying to tell you something!"

There was an intensity to the ferret's cries that I had not heard before. Could it be an eep of warning?

"Oops," Richard called down to us. "I think my hours of indecision are over."

"What is the matter?" Norei shouted her concern.

The giant frowned down at her. "Remember that Netherhells battle taking place two valleys over? Well, they're not fighting anymore."

"Indeed," I shouted to him, wishing for some further explanation. "Is everybody gone?"

"No, not everybody." Richard sighed. "Well, I guess it was time to get back to work, anyway. It was fun having freedom while it lasted."

"Doom," Hendrek interjected, as the Seven Other Dwarves explained the giant's behavior in song:

> "Ho hack, ho hack,
>   Mother Duck is back!"

So that was what my ferret was trying to tell me! Beloved pet that he was, he had left us to watch Mother Duck, so that he might warn us if she had won the battle.

"Good ferret!" I enthused. "Excellent ferret!"

"Eep eep!" the ferret answered happily. "Eep eep eep!"

"Then we are surely doomed to a life of fairy tales!" Smarmy wailed.

"Indeed," I replied calmly. "I think not."

"Doom," Hendrek remarked, shifting his deadly warclub from hand to hand. "Then it is not too late to fight?"

"Not at all. Rather, it is not too late to run." I pointed at the nearby warning signs. "We are already on the edge of the Eastern Kingdoms. I suggest we begin traveling out of them, as of now."

And travel we did. After all, I had learned more than a few simple spells from the greatest wizard in the Western Kingdoms.

I had learned all about escape routes as well.

FIVE

Giants (see figure 346B) are your friends. Anything that large is your friend. Trust me. And if you find out I'm wrong, you can always will this book to your next of kin.

—From *Ebenezum's Handy Guide to Woodland Creatures*
(with accompanying illustrations), fourth edition,
by Ebenezum,
greatest wizard in the Western Kingdoms

I scooped up the crystal ball as I ran from the clearing into the woods. In the distance, I could hear a woman's voice.

"Richard, I see you! Come back here, you coward!"

"Oops!" Richard answered. A great cloud appeared over me and my companions. I didn't realize until it fell to earth a quarter mile in front of us that it was the giant's foot. Richard was running with us.

"Wuntvor!" Norei called from my side. "Where are we going?"

"Back toward Vushta!" I replied. "At least for the time being."

"Doom," Hendrek interjected from where he lumbered at Norei's side. "The time being?"

41

I nodded. "Until we can think of a better way to rescue Ebenezum."

"Make way!" a magnificent voice shouted as a brilliant blur of white galloped past, twisting suddenly to avoid a tight copse of trees. "It is best that a beast with a beautiful and deadly horn should lead the way."

"Sounds good to me," Snarks sneered from my other side. "That way, none of us will have to listen while the creature preens."

The two other demons were right on our heels, for I could hear the larger of them going on, with drum accompaniment, about "Guxx Unfufadoo, running demon."

"You'll pardon us if we fly on ahead," Hubert called over his flapping wings, "but this retreat seems a bit overcrowded."

"We'll meet you up ahead," Alea added. "In the Central Kingdoms. That way, we'll get a little time alone to practice some new material."

"Wait for that indispensable talking wolf!" shouted a voice some distance behind us. And I could hear other voices, even more distant.

"Hi hort, hi hort,
To bad our legs are short!"

Fainter even than the song of the Seven Other Dwarves was a faraway, out-of-breath eeping. It sounded as if my ferret, after rushing to warn me of Mother Duck, was now too exhausted to escape!

I jiggled the pocket of my jerkin with my free hand.

"Tap!" I called. "It's time for Brownie Power!"

"Now?" The little fellow grabbed the top of the pocket and glared out at me. "Are you sure?"

Tap did not look at all well. He appeared to be shivering—either that, or it was the movement of my pocket bouncing up and down as I jogged. He was entirely the wrong color as well, altogether too green for a Brownie. Of course, that also might be attributable to my jouncing pocket. I frowned at the wee man. Apparently, our recent scrape with Death, combined, perhaps, with the Brownie's current mode of transportation, had had a negative effect on the small fellow.

"That's telling him!" Snarks exclaimed, smiling at Tap's shivering form. "As far as we're concerned, it's never time for Brownie Power!"

"What? Huh?" Tap stood tall, his head clearing the top of my pocket by an inch or more. "No, His Brownieship would never let me back in if I think like that." He took a deep breath. "A Brownie must be ever alert, ever vigilant and ever ready to make shoes. That's part of the Brownie Creed! Where do you need Brownie Power? I'm ready now!"

"How noble!" Norei remarked with her beautiful smile.

"Doom!" Hendrek rumbled. "What self-sacrifice!"

"How sickening!" Snarks added.

I ignored all of them as I quickly told the Brownie my plan. There were members of our company who were lagging behind, who might soon be overtaken and once again subjugated by Mother Duck. There was only one way to save them: through the magic of Brownie transportation.

"A difficult job," Tap agreed. "But Brownie Power is up to it! Brownie Power is up to anything!"

"I've personally had Brownie Power up to here," Snarks remarked, but Tap was already gone, vanished with one of those smoke-producing-tiny-explosions he had.

"Richard!" Mother Duck's voice called again. She sounded as if she was drawing closer. How could someone of her advanced years move that quickly?

"Oops!" Richard shouted from some distance up ahead. "Goodbye!" The giant began to run, his first two steps sending tremors that threatened to knock us from our feet. Then he jumped over a low mountain range and disappeared from sight.

"Richard?" Mother Duck's voice protested shrilly. "What am I going to do without a giant? I mean, Jack-the-Very-Tall-Person-Killer simply doesn't sound right. Richard!"

But the giant was gone. And suddenly Mother Duck did not sound quite so close as before. Perhaps she had stopped her pursuit. It was then that I realized that the intervening woods prevented the woman from seeing the rest of us. Maybe she would stop now, exhausted from her earlier battle, and never realize her former victims were within easy recapture. If, somehow, we could increase slightly the distance between us; if, perhaps, we could remain quiet but for a few more moments—

There was a moderate explosion in our midst.

"Eep eep!" the ferret remarked.

"What a way for talking wolves to travel!" Jeffrey complained.

"Hey!" Noisy added enthusiastically. "That was great!"

"No," Tap groaned, falling to his knees. "That was Brownie Power! Eleven at one blow!" He fell face-first into the dirt.

"There's something in these woods, isn't there?" Mother Duck called from some distance behind us.

I quickly stuffed the Brownie back in my pocket.

"Indeed," I suggested. "I don't think we should be out here for long." I picked up the ferret as well, returning the small, furry creature to my pack.

"I hear you!" Mother Duck called somewhat more forcefully than before. "Don't think that you can escape me!"

"Doom," Hendrek rumbled as he glanced over his shoulder. "What should we do now?"

"Run even faster!" I replied, for I had seen a sign up ahead:

YOU ARE NOW ENTERING THE CENTRAL KINGDOMS
THANK YOUR LUCKY STARS!

I did not know if leaving Mother Duck's domain would actually help us. But it certainly wouldn't hurt.

We made it to the sign in a matter of moments, but not without some difficulty. The Seven Other Dwarves gasped behind me as one:

"Ho heth, ho heth,
We are quite out of breath!"

I paused to look behind us. It couldn't be! But it was. I could already see Mother Duck's figure darting rapidly through the trees.

"It's hopeless, you know!" she yelled for our benefit. "Once you visit Mother Duck, you visit her forever!"

The old woman seemed to be running at a speed five times as fast as a normal person. At this rate, she would overtake us in a couple minutes.

"How can she—" I began.

"In Mother Duck's kingdom"—Smarmy wheezed—"Mother Duck can do anything."

"Doom," Hendrek pointed out. "But we are no longer in Mother Duck's kingdom."

"Exactly," Norei stated, pulling back her sleeves to give her hands more room to conjure. "Allow me."

She made a rapid series of passes through the air, followed by a quick string of words of power. And the woods between us and Mother Duck started to grow.

Trees sprouted new branches pointing toward the ground, while bushes doubled their height in the blink of an eye. Dead leaves spread upon the ground turned green again and sent shoots into the soft earth, turning into a field of strong young saplings before us. Snarks yelled in surprise as his stout oak staff took root in the dirt between his feet, while the rest of us gasped in awe as the "You are now entering the Central Kingdoms" sign sprouted a hundred tiny branches, spreading from the square of wood like ripples from a pond, and completing, in concert with the trees and bushes, an impenetrable wall of vegetation.

"Not bad, huh?" Norei allowed.

"Indeed!" I enthused, looking at my beloved with renewed admiration. "What a wonderful spell!"

Norei blushed, the color on her cheeks making her even more beautiful than before. " 'Twas not all that special. Naught but a simple wild-agricultural-growth spell, slightly amended to allow for forest conditions."

"Doom," Hendrek interjected. "But will it stop Mother Duck?"

"I think it has a chance," Norei answered. "You see, if the spell has worked properly, it has not only formed the impenetrable forest wall that you see before you. In addition, the magic should continue to replicate itself upon the other side, causing the dense growth to push into the Eastern Kingdoms, straight for Mother Duck. She will have to stop that part of the spell first before she can hope to clear a path through this enchanted forest to reach us." My beloved paused, taking a deep breath. "I may not be able to stop Mother Duck, but I can certainly slow her down."

"Very impressive," Snarks commented. "Why didn't you do it before?"

But the demon's query didn't phase the beautiful witch in the least.

"Before," she replied, "we were in the Eastern Kingdoms, a locale that seems to increase Mother Duck's sorceries while dampening all other magicks. Now, however, we are beyond the influence of her spells. Outside of her kingdom, I imagine the two of us are more or less equals. And, this time, I had surprise on my side."

"Indeed," I beamed at my beloved. "Then what shall we do now?"

Norei smiled at me, dimpling prettily. "I suggest we resume running. My spell will not contain Mother Duck forever."

"Indeed!" I called to the others. "Let's go then, as quick as we can!"

We continued our flight at a brisk trot. The greater the distance we put between ourselves and Mother Duck, I reasoned, the more chance we had of escaping her altogether. Then, with any luck, we would catch up with Hubert and Alea, and perhaps even Richard the giant.

But what should we do after we rendezvoused with the others? Perhaps, as we continued to move quickly, I should try to contact my master.

I looked at the crystal ball, which I had been carrying all the while in my hand. But where had I put the incantation?

I excused myself as I reached into my pocket, but the Brownie was sound asleep, exhausted from his earlier exertions. I managed to find the parchment tucked behind him and, with some little difficulty, drew it forth. I shook the paper open with a flick of my wrist and once again read the magic words:

> "Secret sphere, seashore seer,
> Surely showing sunshine seeking . . ."

I had to read it "quickly and in a loud voice" according to the directions.

"Secret sphere," I began, "sheshore sheer—" No, that wasn't quite right, was it?"

"Oh, dear," Snarks remarked solicitously. "Are you developing a stutter?"

"Doom," Hendrek replied forcefully. "He is using the crystal ball. Let him be."

Everyone around me quieted, waiting. The hush made me a little nervous. What if nothing happened?

I rushed through the incantation as best I could.

"Well?" Snarks asked at the conclusion of the rhyme.

"Doom," Hendrek rumbled again. "Give him time."

"Look!" Norei pointed to the crystal. "Something's happening!"

And it was. The globe, once transparent, was now filled with a gray mist, upon which I could see flashes of yellow light. But it was more than mere pyrotechnics, for the light formed itself into letters, and the letters into words.

"There is a message!" I announced, and proceeded to read aloud:

"We are," the message began, words swirling through the mist for an instant and then gone, "sorry, but we are unable . . . to complete your call . . . as spoken . . . Please release . . . the crystal . . . and try again."

"You call that a message?" Snarks asked.

"Doom," Hendrek began, but I waved them both to silence.

"Indeed," I remarked. "It is my own fault, for trying to conjure in flight. I fear I cannot run and read at the same time. I will use the crystal ball again when we stop to rest." Whenever that might be.

A loud voice hailed us from up ahead, where the forest ended at a towering cliff face.

"Hey, folks! It's us: the lady who wows all the males and the reptile with the winning scales!"

I would recognize that patter anywhere. It was Damsel and Dragon. I waved to the large purplish-blue reptile. Perhaps, when we reached them and regrouped, I would get a moment's respite to reuse the crystal.

"Oops!" an even louder voice remarked. Richard the giant peeked out from around the cliff face. "I was hiding."

"Indeed!" I shouted ahead. " 'Tis a pleasure to see you!" Now that we had left Mother Duck behind, having a giant on our side could be nothing but a boon.

"Once I jumped over the mountain, I circled around," the giant confided. "Mother Duck will never find me now!"

But another voice, clear yet distant, was carried by the breeze.

"Richard, you coward!" the woman screamed. "You won't escape me again!"

SIX

Always make the best use of your resources. Magic, escape routes, hungry demons, annoying in-laws: All can be used constructively by the creative wizard. And should you add, say, an irate client who is annoyed that an unforeseen side effect of your most recent spell has turned his wife into a chicken, well, I'm sure I don't have to tell you that the possibilities for combinations are almost limitless.

—From *No Bad Wizards:*
A Study of Sorcerers and How to Train Them,
fourth edition,
by Ebenezum,
greatest wizard in the Western Kingdoms

"Oops," Richard remarked.

"Doom," Hendrek answered.

"Run!" I commanded. "If need be, to the Inland Sea!"

But then I had another thought as the rest of our party took off at a brisk trot. It had taken us a good two days to reach the Eastern Kingdoms from Vushta. There was no way we could run all the way back. I looked up at our very large companion.

"Richard, might you wait a minute?"

The giant paused mid-stride. "But Mother Duck—" he protested.

"Indeed," I replied. "I fear she might dog our footsteps forever, unless we devise a plan. She moved with astonishing speed when still in her kingdom. Even now, I imagine, she probably follows us with a pace and agility amazing for one of her advanced years. But how can any old lady, no matter how magically inclined, hope to catch up with a giant?"

"Oops," Richard responded. "I beg your pardon?"

"If you start now," I explained patiently, "you will easily outdistance Mother Duck. I imagine you could outdistance anyone, except for other giants."

Richard nodded, still dumbfounded.

I continued: "But Mother Duck is magical enough so that she might be able to overtake the rest of us, and once again subjugate us to her will."

"Doom," Hendrek interjected from some fifty paces ahead.

"And that would leave you without your newfound companions," I further explained, "who are here to help you find new direction in the world beyond the Eastern Kingdoms."

The giant nodded again, his forehead slowly uncreasing.

"I see you, Richard!" Mother Duck called again, this time louder, and closer, than before. "Wait until I get my spells on you!"

"Oops!" Richard commented with some consternation, frowning in the direction of the Eastern Kingdoms.

"Ignore her," I informed the giant. "If there was some way she could have affected you at this distance, she would have done so already."

"If you say so," the giant replied without much conviction in his voice.

"Indeed," I responded with my most reassuring tone. "As I was saying—if you are left alone, or we are left without you, we shall all surely once again fall prey to Mother Duck. But there is another way—a way we can combine your speed and our cunning—and that's if you pick us up and take us with you."

"Oops!" Richard smiled slowly, rather like a shadow creeping across the full moon. "What a good idea!" He began to pat various parts of his pants legs, producing sounds not unlike thunder echoing in the mountains.

"Indeed," I prompted. "Then my plan will work?"

"Oops," Richard answered. "It will if I have enough pockets." He gave up examining his pants and laid his hand, palm up, across half the field-size clearing. "Climb aboard."

I did as I was bade and, a moment later, found myself tucked in the giant's shirt pocket.

Richard took a tiny step forward so that he stood directly behind our fleeing company.

"Hey!" Snarks shouted with alarm. "Watch your feet!"

"Oops," Richard rumbled, but I cut him off, quickly explaining, in as loud a voice as I could muster, my plans to the others.

"Oh, my clever Wuntvor!" Norei enthused. Even though I was quite some distance away, I could still imagine the sweet smile upon her lovely face. I wondered for an instant if there was some way to discreetly ask Richard to place the young witch in the same pocket with me.

The dwarves cheered as well:

"Hi hicket, hi hicket,
That Wuntvor's just the ticket!"

Everyone else, with the possible exception of Guxx, seemed generally in favor of the plan. Even Hendrek's "Doom" sounded somewhat more cheerful than usual.

"Don't you go anywhere, Richard!" Mother Duck's ever-more-forceful voice called from somewhere not all that far to our rear.

"Commence!" Guxx commanded his drum-wielding cohort. Brax beat, but both were scooped up immediately by Richard, and any further drum beating and declamation was soon lost behind the thick fabric of the giant's britches.

Richard hurriedly picked up the remaining members of my retinue, stuffing them in various pockets upon his person. There was some grumbling among the companions, especially when Snarks found he was going to have to share pocket space with the unicorn, while Jeffrey exclaimed that someone with the stature of a talking wolf should surely be shown to a pocket above the belt. Still, only Hubert refused to be carried away, saying it would be better for all concerned if he and Alea flew on ahead.

"Indeed," I remarked as Richard pocketed the last of the dwarves in a small denim envelope slightly above his knee. "If we are all tucked firmly away—"

"If you know what's good for you, Richard," Mother Duck's very forceful voice interrupted, "you'll stand there until I get a little closer!"

"Oops!" Richard replied as he took off at an earthshaking pace.

We reached the Inland Sea in a little under three minutes. Richard stopped abruptly on the shore.

"Pardon me," he murmured, "but I'm a little afraid of water."

I assured the giant it was quite all right, and pointed to Vushta in the near distance. We were surrounded by silence, the only sounds the lapping of the waves by Richard's feet and the screams of gulls circling his brow. We had left Mother Duck far behind.

"Indeed," I said at last, reluctantly breaking into the first peaceful moment we had experienced since the heavens knew when. "It is perhaps time to place my companions and myself back on the ground. If we are all to proceed to Vushta, I believe it is advisable that I lead the way to provide the introductions."

"Oops," Richard nodded in understanding. "Unintroduced giants tend to bring out the worst in people."

The giant proceeded to unload us all from his various pockets.

"Begin!" Guxx screamed as he hit the ground. This time, he would not be denied.

> "Guxx Unfufadoo, dissheveled demon,
>   Does not belong in giant's pocket;
>   Has words to say to those who'll listen!
>   Those that don't will feel his anger!"

"The big fellow couldn't be the slightest bit annoyed?" Snarks ventured.

"And justifiably so!" Jeffrey snapped. "Here he is, the former ruler of the Netherhells, and he got a pocket even lower than mine."

"Indeed!" I said, hoping to halt this line of conversation before it became another full-fledged argument. Guxx Unfufadoo, the former Grand Hoohah (whatever that was) of all the Netherhells, was used to being obeyed, feared and fled from. He was not used to being ignored; and that was what my companions and I had been doing ever since Death arrived upon the scene. Still, there was no time to lose. Was there some way to assuage this demon's anger while we went about finding a way to save my master?

"Continue!" Guxx roared.

> "Guxx Unfufadoo, annoyed demon,
> Will stand no more of this abusive
> Treatment that's unfit for heroes,
> Wants a say in future ventures!"

Oh, dear. This was worse than I thought. Guxx wanted a say in our decision making? Somehow, I had to quiet the demon down now.

"Indeed," I began again. But now that he had gotten started, Guxx would let no one interrupt.

"Amplify!" he shrieked. Brax beat the drum even more vigorously.

> "Guxx Unfufadoo, angered demon,
> Has decided to speak loudly
> Will decree that all shall listen,
> Will stand alone as Wuntvor's partner!"

Stand alone? Wuntvor's partner? Guxx flexed his long, razor-sharp claws to punctuate his demands. His statements were becoming more outrageous with every declamation. But what could I do to stop them?

"There you are!" Hubert the dragon called from some-where above. "It's taken us a minute to catch up with you. I must say, Richard, when you want to move, you move!"

"Oops," Richard agreed.

Hubert swooped down to land.

"Overwhelm!" the former Grand Hoohah bellowed.

"Guxx Unfufadoo, outraged demon—"

"Someone's declaiming?" Hubert remarked brightly as he landed. "Does that mean it's time for a little musical number?"

"Has no time for—
   Musical number?"

Guxx's voice died in his throat.

"Indeed," I insisted to both demon and dragon. "No."

I looked about at my remaining companions. "There are obviously many issues that must be resolved concerning our quest. However, I should suggest that, rather than pausing to discuss our problems in the wild, it would be much better to debate them in the much safer confines of the College of Wizards in Vushta."

"Wuntvor?" Norei said softly. "Might I make a suggestion?"

I asked her to proceed.

"I was wondering," she remarked gently, "should we go to Vushta? There might be a few problems. The city might be full of wizards, but when we left them, they were all sneezing."

"Indeed," I replied, giving myself a moment to think, something that had been virtually impossible during our recent flight and subsequent demon declaiming. As usual, my beloved was all too correct. My master's malady had been passed on to the other wizards of Vushta, a malady that caused each and every wizard to sneeze violently when confronted by a mystic spell or a magical being. They had had enough trouble before, with unicorns and demons in their midsts. I shuddered now to think how the amassed noses of greater Vushta would react if we brought a giant among them.

Worse still, I had been sent by these amassed wizards to the Eastern Kingdoms to enlist the aid of Mother Duck in our fight against the Netherhells and, if possible, to see if she might know of a cure for the wizards' affliction. How would the magicians feel now if I returned to them empty-handed?

It was a quandary. I glanced about at my fellows, wondering if any of them could offer the advice I needed. But the one man whose wisdom was sorely needed was not among us. I sighed.

What would my master do?

I thought about the dwarves' gift, now safely tucked away in my pack. Mother Duck was miles behind, and Death seemed unlikely to make an appearance so close to a place teaming with life as the City of a Thousand Forbidden Delights. Perhaps it was time once again to consult the crystal ball.

"Indeed," I said to the others. "You have brought up weighty matters. It is time, perhaps, to consult powers greater than my own."

I opened the pack and, after pausing briefly to pet the ferret, extracted the globe. I reached into my pocket and nudged past the still-sleeping Brownie to retrieve the folded piece of parchment. I silently reread the incantation:

> Secret sphere, seashore seer,
> Surely showing sunshine seeking.
> Simply said, the shaft is shed,
> Spouting spells that send us shrieking.

I took a deep breath. It was now or never. But I would say the words more carefully than before, cautious to avoid the strange message I received when I first attempted to use the mystic crystal. Perhaps it wouldn't be as quickly spoken as the incantation instructions urged, but I would manage somehow.

And manage I did, on only the third try. I peered, deep within the magic ball.

There was something happening! In fact, I could hear voices! I brought the milky globe close to my ear so that I might better discern the words. The one speaking now had a high and brittle tone, like that of a woman of advanced years. Yes! I understood her quite clearly now:

"Then I said to the swami, 'If you call that fortune-telling, I've got some swampland I could sell—' Hey, who's that?"

So the mystic globe discerned my presence! But how should I address this magic ball? Politely, I decided after a moment, but directly.

"Indeed," I replied deferentially. "I am Wuntvor the apprentice. I'm trying to reach my master, the great wizard Ebenezum."

"He is Wuntvor the apprentice, trying to reach the great wizard," the voice mimicked. "Hey, don't you know this is a party crystal? What do you mean, eavesdropping on my conversation?"

"Party crystal?" I replied. "Eavesdropping?" But I could concoct no coherent reply. I could only think of one thing: that this woman would keep me from reaching my master!

"But madam!" I pleaded. "It is a matter of life or death!"

"Life, smife," the voice snorted. "That's what they all say. Well, I'll have you know that Mabel and I haven't had a good conversation in over a week!"

"But Vushta—" I sputtered. "Sneezing wizards! Imminent demon attacks from the Netherhells! My master, trapped in the Kingdom of the Dead!"

"What is this, a nuisance call?" The voice in the crystal was getting annoyed. "There's no need to get uppity. And there's no reason for you to feel put out. If you can't stand to wait your turn, you should have gotten yourself a private ball. Now, go away! I have a conversation to finish. —So, anyways, the Swami says to me, 'How dare you! A curse upon your firstborn!' Well, Mabel, I just had to laugh. You know how my eldest is, always taking his mother for granted. Maybe, I thought, if he has a curse on him, he'll write to me for a change—"

It was hopeless. I placed the glass globe back in my sack. What should I do?

The wind was picking up. Sand whipped up from the beach, stinging my face. I worried about this sudden change in the weather.

Death often announced itself with the wind. Did I hear some sounds carried by this stiffening breeze, sounds like boulders being ground to dust? No, that wasn't quite it. There was something else there instead, something faint, a woman's voice calling a single name.

Richard.

I shivered. It seemed as if Death was near, and Mother Duck wasn't far behind.

"Sounds pretty bad," Snarks agreed as he stepped forward from my companions. "That crazy old lady is coming for the giant, and it looks like we might get another visit from the death of the party. There's no way we can go back to Vushta, 'cause we flubbed the quest. And let's face it, it wasn't even much of a quest in the first place. And then there's that wizard of yours, but I guess, if you feel you've got to save him, you've got to save him."

I nodded. The demon had, in his own inimitable way, summarized our situation.

"You agree?" Snarks continued. "Very well. I think it's time you listened to me."

"Indeed?" I replied.

The demon nodded in turn, showing his mottled gray teeth in a fiendish smile.

"I have a plan."

SEVEN

There is absolutely no truth to the rumors of impropriety. And those seven women leaving my room in quick succession was simply a coincidence. If you'll excuse me—you're blocking my escape route.

—Further testimony from Ebenezum,
greatest wizard in the Western Kingdoms,
concerning Wizardgate

"Indeed?"

"It has to do with my extensive religious background," the demon confided.

I stared at the small green figure. We had first met the demon when he was part of a small hermetic order that somehow had bent the rules sufficiently so that they not only spoke to other people but charged them to stay overnight at their elaborate hovel. And that order had had a close, personal relationship with a very minor deity.

"Do you mean?" I blurted.

"Yes," Snarks confirmed. "Death believes it has us trapped, for, so long as we are upon this mortal plain, it can surround us at any moment. Even worse, while we are avoiding Death, we might run directly into the extremely annoying Mother Duck. And Vushta cannot save us, for the city is filled with sneezing wizards. There is only one hope. We must appeal to a higher authority. We must contact Plaugg, the moderately glorious!''

"Indeed?" I replied, stunned by the audacity of the demon's suggestion. "But isn't that going to be rather difficult?" I remembered how long it took Plaugg to pay attention the last time.

"Unfortunately correct," Snarks agreed. "Plaugg, praise his just barely illustrious name, might be a semiomnipotent deity, but he isn't a very attentive one. I have a feeling it has something to do with an unhappy homelife. But now is not the time for idle ecclesiastical speculation. It is, rather, time to contact Plaugg.''

The demon sidled even closer to me, speaking in a voice barely above a whisper. "We who worship the intermittently influential gods have a saying: If you can't get the deity to come to you, you'd better go to the deity. Besides, you are in constant danger when on this mortal coil. I suggest, therefore, that you leave this coil for a friendlier clime. And where could you go? You've already gone down once. Now it's time to go up.''

"Up?" I queried, even more flabbergasted than before. "You mean up in the heavens, among the deities?"

Snarks waved away my objections with a flick of a sickly green claw. "Well, surely, that's not such a big deal. Plaugg, bless his modestly exalted being, is pretty low on the ladder up there, I assure you. We should be able to sneak in without any trouble whatsoever.''

"We?" I said. "Sneak in?"

"Simply leave all the fine points to me," Snarks assured me. "And I'm afraid I have to go along. After all, I'm the one with the history of Plaugg worship, praise his reasonably adequate name.''

"Indeed," I commented. I felt I needed a moment to consider this radical suggestion. I folded my arms across my chest in an attempt to protect myself from the increasingly chill breeze.

My beloved stroked my cheek, a gesture I instantly wished she would repeat any number of times. She whispered my name, so common-sounding when spoken by others, but music when it issued from her lips.

"Indeed?" I queried, my throat suddenly dry.

"As surprising as Snarks's suggestion may be," Norei ventured gently, "I fear it may be our only hope." She pointed at the shifting sands: "Look."

I followed her pointing finger and saw the words etched across the beach:

"Wuntvor. You cannot escape."

They were Death's words, formed by his control of the elements. Death was again carried by the wind.

"Doom," Hendrek muttered darkly. "Will this never end?"

But the breeze also carried other things, like the ever-strengthening voice of Mother Duck:

"Richard! Don't you dare move again!"

"Oops," Richard moaned. "Won't I ever get away?"

"Indeed!" I called to the others. "We must act quickly!" But what, I thought, should we do?

"We will need the assistance of the others," Snarks resumed hastily. "Hubert, for one."

"Me?" the dragon said. "This little green person, who cannot even appreciate the fine points of vaudeville, actually wants help from me?"

"Certainly," Snarks replied, for once not answering the large reptile's sarcasm. "We need someone to fly us to heaven."

"To heaven?" Alea questioned nervously. "Are you sure that can be done?"

Snarks smiled. "Trust me."

"Heaven?" Hubert shook his great wings and spouted a gout of flame. "Why not? It's worth a try. Think of the publicity value if it works!"

"And we'll get a brand-new audience besides!" Alea added, convinced by the demon, and dragon.

"Alas," Snarks quickly clarified. "I'm afraid that the damsel will have to stay behind."

"What?" Hubert protested. "And break up the act?"

"There's no room," Snarks explained.

"I could hold on to Wuntie's waist," Alea ventured. "You'd hardly know I was there!"

Snarks shook his sickly green head. "Too much weight."

"Too much weight?" Alea exploded. "Why, you undersized excuse for a—"

"Sorry," the demon interrupted, "but once we go, we have to go in a hurry. We want to get beyond Death's domain as quickly as possible."

"Beyond Death's domain?" Hubert said doubtfully. "I don't think I can fly that fast."

"Oh, I've thought of that, too." Snarks looked up at the giant. "Richard?"

"Oops," the giant replied.

"How are you at tossing things?" the demon asked.

"Well," the giant considered. "My aim's not too good. But I can toss a pretty fair distance."

"The very answer I was looking for. We're going to need you to toss the dragon, with Wuntvor and me strapped on his back, straight up in the air."

"Straight up?" The giant looked doubtfully into the sky. "I'll try."

"Interject!" a gruff voice screamed, accompanied by rapid drumbeats.

> "Guxx Unfufadoo, confused demon,
> Wants to know just what is happening;
> Wants to know how he fits into
> Wuntvor's plan to save his master!"

"Indeed!" I spoke quickly, for I knew that, with Death and Mother Duck nearby, there was no time to waste. "You will have a most important role, Guxx. For, when Hubert, Snarks and I are sent aloft, we will need others down below to lead the rest of my companions to safety. I have decided to appoint Norei the witch as your leader, for her magic might be needed to save you all. However, we will need more than magic to see us through. I therefore pronounce you, Guxx Unfufadoo, as Chief Protector and Keeper of the Claws for my companions. It is now your duty to see that no one comes to harm!"

"Comment!" Guxx commanded.
Brax beat a rapid rhythm.

"Guxx Unfufadoo, honored demon,
Likes to be called the protector;
Enjoys the chance to do some shredding;
Thinks the job's right up his alley!"

"Indeed, I replied, glad that I had at least temporarily satisfied the large demon. I turned to my beloved. "Once we are aloft, I think that Death will no longer bother you. For the time being, at least, he wants only me. Therefore, you need only avoid Mother Duck. I believe the best way to accomplish this is to take the remains of our party back into Vushta, and inform the wizards there as to the—uh—direction my quest has taken. Even in their impaired state, I think that the magic of those wizards, combined with whatever spells you might muster, will easily keep Mother Duck at bay."

"Wuntvor!" Norei enthused. "What a good plan!"

"I like a man who can take control!" Alea agreed.

The Seven Other Dwarves chimed in:

"Hi hense, hi hense,
He makes a lot of sense."

"Doom," Hendrek remarked. "I shall use my mighty warclub Headbasher to smash our way to Vushta if I must, wading waist-deep through the broken, bloody bodies of our foes!"

"And if that doesn't work," Brax interjected, "I have a small but sophisticated selection of previously owned weapons, available at ridiculously marked-down prices to any here who need them. I mean, I'm practically giving them away!"

"And I shall lead them into Vushta as quickly as I can," Norei said as she leaned close to me. Her lips brushed against my nose. "Now go! Get up on that dragon and fly!"

I remembered to breathe. My lungs had stopped all of

their own accord when my beloved's lips had touched my face. I nodded dumbly and staggered over toward the dragon. My nose tingled where Norei had kissed it. Snarks was right behind me, pushing me a bit here and there when I wandered away from the proper path.

"I'll add my services, too," Jeffrey the wolf assured me as I climbed upon Hubert's back. "I'm not averse to eating a foe in the line of duty. And who knows, maybe some of the foes will be pigs—or grandmothers!"

The unicorn trotted up beside Jeffrey as Snarks clambered up behind me. The beast gave a single shake of its blinding white mane.

"I shall use my magnificent golden horn in our defense as well." The unicorn sighed. "It all goes so quickly. Maybe when you get back we might find a quiet corner where you might"—the beast paused meaningfully for a second— "sit—and I might"—it paused again—"lay my— heavy head for a moment upon your—" It paused one more time, almost too overcome to continue. The last word came out as a whisper: "—lap?"

"Indeed," I answered, taken aback by the beast's pitiful sincerity. "Perhaps someday—"

"Leaving so soon?" asked a voice as dry as decaying leaves. Death's voice.

"Go!" Norei demanded. "We'll come up with a way to distract the specter—somehow!"

Death laughed, and I turned to see the skeletal figure standing on the beach, beckoning.

"You do want to see your master again, don't you, Wuntvor? You do want to save your master? Perhaps I should take you now. Perhaps I should take you all now."

"Oh, no, you don't!" exclaimed the imperious tones of Mother Duck. "I saw them first!"

I turned my head the other way. There was Mother Duck, rapidly striding toward us across the sand.

"Indeed," I said to the demon behind me. "I think now would be a good time to take our leave."

"Richard," Snarks called out to the giant, "if you would?"

"Oops," the giant replied, picking Hubert up with both hands. "Here you go!"

Richard grunted as he tossed up in the air with all his might. Hubert shrieked, a mixture of surprise and fright:

"Dragons aren't supposed to go this fast!"

I craned my neck to look behind. Richard and my other companions disappeared in the distance before I could blink.

"Oh, boy!" Snarks cheered. "We're really flying now! Nobody can stop us anymore!"

I clutched the dragon's scales for dear life. I was all too afraid that the demon was right.

EIGHT

What do you mean, wizards cannot foretell the future? While it may be true that some of us are not as skilled at prophesying as certain other mythological professionals who make that sort of thing their life's work, still your average mage is quite adept at looking into times to come. An example? If you insist. I see through the power of my mystic might that you shall grow older, and so shall I. We shall have our good days, and not so good days. You want something more specific? Very well. I see something happening to you any minute now, something that you cannot avoid.

You will soon have a wizard collecting his fee.
— From *Wizardhood*
(Wizard's Digest Condensed Edition), fourth edition,
by Ebenezum,
greatest wizard in the Western Kingdoms

I had remarked before that things sometimes seemed to go too fast for me. This was the first time, however, that I feared they were going too fast for everyone.

"Weehah!" Snarks whooped behind me. "This is the

way to travel! You know, you'd have to spend good
money to go on a ride like this down in the Netherhells!"

I might have been better able to appreciate the demon's
point of view if the dragon who carried us hadn't been
screaming so much. Getting away from the twin threats of
Death and Mother Duck had seemed of paramount importance but an instant before, and, the heavens knew, Richard's muscular toss had certainly gotten us on our way.
However, having one's mode of transportation constantly
subject to shrieking fits did tend to put a damper on one's
confidence. I did my best to hang on, hoping that things
would calm down eventually.

And slow down we did, after what seemed to be an
eternity.

"Oh, thank goodness!" Hubert exclaimed as he unfolded his wings and flapped them gently to stabilize our
flight. "Wind resistance has brought us under control."

"Do we have to slow down?" Snarks whined. "This is
the most fun I've had since skinny-dipping in the slime
pits!"

"Indeed," I interjected, trying to put the whole thing
into perspective. "I feel it was for the best that we got
away from the situation down below as quickly as possible. Now, however, that we have achieved some distance
from our initial danger, perhaps it is time to fly at a more
reasonable, controlled speed, so that we might modify our
direction to better meet our goal."

"Awww!" Snarks complained.

"A brilliant speech!" Hubert commented. "Have you
ever thought of going into politics? Or perhaps the even
more difficult field of theater management?"

"His explanations are certainly long-winded enough!"
the demon agreed.

"But your recent declaration brings up a small problem," Hubert continued, choosing to ignore Snarks.

"Indeed?" I replied. "Well, whatever it is, I'm sure
we can work it out among us."

"That's right!" Snarks enthused. "I'm the Plaugg worshipper around here, praise his ever so vaguely noble
name."

"Well," the dragon went on a bit sheepishly. "You mentioned direction? You mentioned control?"

"Indeed?" I prompted.

"Well, both of them are good and noble goals," the dragon went on. "But neither is much use if you don't know where you're going." Hubert cleared his throat, producing a fair quantity of smoke. "Uh, where exactly is heaven, anyways?"

I glanced back at my small green companion.

"That is not the sort of question you should ask a demon," Snarks answered a bit huffily.

"Weren't you the one who was supposed to be the expert on Plaugg?" I reminded the demon.

Snarks nodded. "Praise his marginally magnificent name. I always assumed that heaven was—you know—up. But I'm not the expert here. Hubert's the one who's put in all the flying time."

"Hey," the dragon interjected. "I'm in entertainment, not tourism. If you wanted a travel itinerary, you should have consulted my brother Morty."

"Morty?" Snarks asked.

"What's the matter with Morty?" Hubert bristled. "It's a perfectly good dragon name. Perhaps not as distinctive as Hubert, but then, how many names are?"

"I refuse to answer that question at this great a height," Snarks responded.

"Indeed," I interjected once again. "I'm afraid this line of discourse is getting us nowhere near our goal. There must be some way we can find heaven!"

"I can't fly up forever," Hubert agreed. "My wings will get tired."

"So what do you want?" Snarks remarked derisively. "A crystal ball?"

"Indeed?" I remarked, with renewed enthusiasm. "I *have* a crystal ball! Snarks?" I pointed to the pack on my back. "If you would?"

"You call *that* thing a crystal ball?" the demon replied. "Well, I suppose, if I must."

I heard the rustle of fabric as Snarks opened my pack.

"Eep eep! Eep eep eep!"

"Yowp!" Snarks exclaimed. "This thing is booby-trapped!"

I apologized to the demon. I had forgotten about my watch-ferret. I suggested that perhaps it would be better if Snarks pulled the pack from my back and handed it to me.

"Gladly," the demon answered as he gingerly handed the pack, once again closed, over my shoulder so that I could get a firm grip on it.

"Tell me," Snarks added. "Do you always keep small animals tucked amidst your clothing?"

"Indeed," I replied, opening the pack for myself. "You never know when they'll come in handy."

"Eep!" the ferret responded. I petted the small furry creature for a moment, then retrieved the magic crystal.

"Here goes nothing," I murmured rhetorically as I reached in my pocket for the incantation.

"You can say that again," Snarks murmured back.

There was a lump in my pocket. I had quite forgotten, in my haste to get away, that I had had a sleeping Brownie upon my person; and did, in fact, still have a sleeping Brownie nestled in my pocket. I pulled the directions from behind the fellow's inert form. Tap muttered something about shoes.

I held the crystal ball with my right hand, the incantation with my left. But now that I once again had the magic sphere, what should I do with it? Should I attempt to contact Plaugg? But what if a crystal of this sort could not speak with a deity, no matter how minor? I had had enough trouble with this mystic device already to discourage me from further experimentation. No, I should use this glass globe for its original purpose, to contact my master in the Kingdom of the Dead. Ebenezum would know the way to heaven. My master knew almost everything.

"Now, no talking, please," I warned the demon. "I must concentrate so that the spell will work correctly."

Snarks, seemingly on the verge of adding a comment or two, only nodded.

Very well. I read the incantation once more:

"Secret sphere, seashore seer,
Surely showing sunshine seeking.
Simply said, the shaft is shed,
Spouting spells that send us shrieking."

I gazed deep within the crystal ball. Ebenezum, I thought, let me contact Ebenezum.

There were no voices this time warning me away, nor messages that I had misspoken the spell. This time I would get through! I gazed intently at the globe, which was suddenly filled with a dense smoke. From somewhere, I heard a distant ringing, then an audible click.

After a moment's silence, the ringing began again, fainter than the first time. Then another click, and nothing. I thought I might have heard even fainter voices through the silence, but their conversation was not loud enough for me to make out the words. At last, the ball clicked again, followed by a ringing so quiet that it was barely discernible. I realized how far the powers of this globe had to reach to contact the Kingdom of the Dead. I began to feel that the crystal's search for my master might take forever.

There was another click, another moment of silence, and then a voice began to speak, faint but discernible. It was not my master's voice, but that of a stranger! What could this mean? It spoke quickly, in clipped, impersonal tones, and I listened carefully, fearful of what it might tell me about Ebenezum:

"All mystic circuits are busy at the present time. Please put down your crystal and try again later."

"Oof!" Hubert remarked. Snarks and I were jostled forcibly as the dragon's feet connected with something solid. The crystal ball flew from my hands, and was lost almost instantly in the cloud bank that surrounded us. Apparently, we had landed somewhere.

"My ball!" I shouted after the recently disappeared device.

"No great loss," Snarks replied.

To my surprise, I found that I agreed with the demon.

Hubert swiveled his head about to regard the two of us.

"Excuse me, fellows, but I simply had to take a breather."

"Indeed," I said, looking at our cloud-shrouded surroundings. "Do you have any idea where we are?"

"Of course," Hubert replied confidently. "Up here is dragon territory. I brought us to the second highest peak in the world, and someplace that we might get some information.

"Indeed?" I answered, doing my best to discern anything in our vicinity save the never-ending grayness. "There are habitations hereabouts?"

There are more than simple habitations," the dragon sniffed dramatically. "We are near the home of the Three Fates. They can tell us everything we need to know"—he paused for effect—"and perhaps a few things we might wish to stay ignorant of."

"Doom," Snarks intoned. I glanced back at the small green demon.

"Hey," he shrugged. "Hendrek may be stuck down below, but he's with us in spirit."

"Indeed," I replied. "Hubert, if you will lead us to the Fates?"

"No need," the dragon answered. "The Fates shall find us."

And with that, as if the fates had been listening, the weather changed dramatically. The fog burned away in an instant, and we found ourselves upon a sun-drenched, windswept mountainside, a hundred yards away from an imposing building made of shining black stone.

"The Temple of the Fates," Hubert explained.

"Who seeks the wisdom of the fates?" a woman's voice called.

"Three humble travelers," I shouted back, "searching for the way to heaven!"

"A worthy goal!" the woman replied. "You may approach the temple!"

"Indeed," I whispered to the others. "Perhaps Snarks and I should dismount. I don't know if riding into a temple like this on a dragon would be considered proper etiquette."

Neither of my companions disagreed, so the demon and I slid from the dragon's back and walked up the gentle mountain slope to the imposing edifice. We mounted the building's first step.

"You may enter!" the voice cried from within. "And we will answer three questions—no more, no less—although we do apologize for being a little short-handed at the moment."

I took the final two steps quickly, and entered the building through a great, round portal. The walls within were of the deepest black, yet somehow glistened with an eerie light. I heard Snarks at my heels, as our two sets of feet thumped across the marble-hard floors.

"Turn," two voices spoke as one, "and face the Fates."

I did as I was told, and saw from the corner of my eye that Hubert had stuck his head into the portal behind us. What I saw next, though, caused me to stop all movement whatsoever, save the opening of my mouth.

Two women stood on adjoining pedestals, if women they truly were. For they wore long robes, perhaps of gray, or perhaps of white or black, or perhaps of every color at once or no color at all. They were tall and lithe, with long-fingered hands and delicate feet, and long hair cascading across their shoulders, although the tresses also resisted any categorization as to color or texture.

But I could accept their hair and clothing readily enough. What really surprised me were their faces—if that was what you could call the orbs that sat atop their shoulders. Not that their heads did not have eyes, noses, ears and mouths, but that they had too many. But that did not explain it, either, for at any moment one of their faces would only hold two eyes, one nose, one mouth. It was just that one instant the eyes would be small and blue, and then change to a pair that was large and black, and then transform again to green and almond-shaped. The mouth, the nose, the cheeks, the chin, every part of the face, would likewise re-form, so that one visage would be replaced by another totally new, completely different. And it happened so quickly, one likeness, then another, and a fourth, a fifth, an eighth, a tenth; the features fled across their faces like clouds across the sun. It was as if their faces were the face of every woman in the world, perhaps every woman who had ever lived or would ever live. But after a moment I realized that even that was too simple, for the faces were too many and varied; there were men there as well, and children; everyone young and old, every shape and size and color.

These, I thought, were the Fates.

The one on the left inclined her head.

"I am Victoria."

The one on the right bowed slightly.

"And I am Mary Jane. We are the Two Fates."

"Normally," Victoria added, "we are the Three Fates. Unfortunately, our sister, Hortense, is not with us at the moment. She is—" The fate hesitated, unable to continue.

"On vacation," her sister fate finished for her. "She complained of overwork."

"Being a fate can be trying at times," Victoria admitted. "Still—"

"Oh, come, now," Mary Jane chided. "Hortense was becoming really frazzled. She needed a break—"

"The Fates watch over all eternity!" Victoria exclaimed. "How can you take a break from that?"

"It's all a matter of attitude," Mary Jane insisted. "I'm sure Hortense went somewhere warm and sunny and quiet. Although I do wish she'd drop us a line."

"But we are making our petitioners wait!" Victoria reminded her sister. She waved graciously at me and my companions. "Our petty little squabbles should not affect you. At least, I hope they don't affect you very much."

"What else can we do?" Mary Jane asked. "We'd best get on with it."

"Very well." Victoria sighed. "Remember, we shall answer three questions—no more, no less! So ask, mortals, and the Fates shall reply. She looked to Mary Jane, who nodded in response. The Two Fates climbed onto adjoining platforms, leaving a third pedestal empty.

"Indeed," I answered, for I wanted to make sure it was

I who asked the questions. I thought for an instant what I should ask first, but that answer was obvious. I had to ask the fates what the crystal ball had failed to tell me.

"How shall I find my master, the great wizard Ebenezum?"

"Here is the answer!" Victoria and Mary Jane shouted in unison.

"If ye shall seek the land of Death," Victoria began.

"And carefully ye save your breath—" Mary Jane continued.

This was followed by silence. The fates looked at us expectantly.

"That's it?" Snarks demanded.

"Is that your second question?" the fates asked in unison.

"Indeed, no!" I hastily interjected. "Snarks was but remarking on the nature of your prophecy, for it seemed somehow incomplete."

"I'm afraid so," Victoria agreed. "Usually, there is a third line that completes the prophecy, but with Hortense gone—"

"Quite right," Mary Jane continued. "There's no one here to finish our prediction!"

"Indeed!" I said. "But couldn't one of you recite the third line?"

"Indeed not!" Mary Jane chided.

"Entirely out of the question!" Victoria sniffed. "There is a precise division of labor here, and we don't want to step on any toes. Each fate recites one third of the prophesy—no more, no less."

"That's how we've always done it," Mary Jane agreed, "and it's how we always will do it. After all, we fates have to live with one another throughout eternity!"

"Indeed." I pondered this new problem. "Let me ask you this—not officially, mind you—what if I were to ask you that same question a second time? Could one of you then deliver the missing portion of the prophecy?"

"Oh, my, no," Mary Jane murmured. "What an absurd idea."

"I'm afraid not," Victoria added more solemnly. "Prophecy is a tricky thing, you see. It's all based on the inspiration of the moment. If we don't get it the first time, it's lost forever.''

"So that's all we get?" Snarks demanded. "Two thirds of a prophecy?"

"Well," Mary Jane huffed. "You needn't take that attitude!"

"I should say so!" Victoria added. "What you received is certainly better than no prophecy at all!"

"It is?" Snarks replied, not at all convinced.

"Why, of course!" Victoria insisted.

"Prophecies are always stated in the form of rhyming riddles, anyway," Mary Jane added.

"Quite correct," Victoria added. "So this riddle is simply a bit more difficult than those we usually speak. But the problem shouldn't be insurmountable."

"Exactly!" Mary Jane enthused. "Especially with the rhyme scheme of the first two lines. Now, let's see, my prediction was 'And carefully ye save your breath—' ''

"And mine was 'If ye shall seek the land of Death,' '' Victoria added.

"So discovering the third line should be simplicity itself!" Mary Jane smiled with her many mouths. "Simply think of something that rhymes with breath and death!"

But Victoria frowned. "Actually, there isn't all that much that rhymes with breath and death."

The fate was quite correct in that assumption. I could think of no rhymes at all.

"It could be breath or death again," Mary Jane added uncertainly. "Rhyming's tricky that way."

"Indeed!" I remarked, trying hard to keep despair from my voice. "Is there no other rhyme?"

"Of course there is!" Hubert rumbled from where his head rested on the portal. "Shibboleth!"

"Shibboleth?" Snarks asked.

"A legitimate word," Victoria responded.

"Quite possibly the answer," Mary Jane added. "Let's see:

> "If ye shall seek the land of Death,
> And carefully ye save your breath,
> Da da da da da shibboleth!"

She nodded, quite pleased with herself. "I don't see why not."

"I came upon the word in my experience in the legitimate theater," the dragon explained proudly. "You learn a great deal when you trod the boards with true thespians!"

"Indeed," I queried, "what does the word mean?"

"Mean? Shibboleth?" The dragon puffed a pensive plume of smoke. "The theater is a hectic place. I barely have time to learn my lines. You can't expect me to understand them as well!"

"Don't look at me," Snarks added. "We didn't have any shibboleths at all in the Netherhells—unless there were some hiding in the slime pits."

I turned to the Fates.

"Do you perchance know the meaning of the word?"

"Is that your second question?" the Two Fates replied as one.

"No, no, certainly not!" I insisted. "The second question is something entirely different." I studied the two women for a moment. "Before I ask that second question, however, I do have the slightest procedural inquiry. I gather, from our earlier discussion, that that sort of question is allowed?"

The fates glanced at each other, their flickering faces twin masks of thought.

Victoria turned to look at me first. "Well, in this case, I suppose so."

Mary Jane nodded. "With Hortense gone, we do have to bend the rules a little."

"Very well," I replied, pointing at the pedestals on which they stood. "It appears that what part of the prophecy you speak is dependent on your positions on those platforms?"

"Very astute," Victoria remarked. "We always foretell left to right."

"Indeed," I answered. "Therefore, since the two of you are standing on the left-hand and central pillars, you will be able to tell me the first two thirds of my prophecy!"

"You're very good at this!" Mary Jane said brightly. "You know, with a mind like that, you could apply yourself and guess that riddle!"

"Indeed," I said. "Perhaps in a few minutes. First, I need to ask a boon."

"A boon?" Victoria frowned.

"We usually don't do those," Mary Jane explained. "We tend to specialize in questions."

"I realize that," I replied, maintaining my patience as I had seen my master maintain his a hundred times before. "But this is a small boon, and would cause you little trouble. I simply ask, if you please, if Mary Jane would move from the central pedestal to that on the right? Then, when I ask a question, I should be able to get both the beginning and the end of your prophecy."

The fates looked at each other again.

"I suppose so—"

"Do you think Hortense would—"

"Why would she care? She's off sunning herself someplace!"

"Very well, mortal," the two of them answered in unison. " 'Tis the least we can do."

Mary Jane stepped over to the right-hand pillar. Victoria waited a moment while her sister smoothed her robes. Then both turned to face me and my companions. Mary Jane spoke next:

"Now we shall answer two questions—no more, no less. Ask mortals, and the fates shall reply!"

"Indeed," I said again. But what should I ask? Perhaps, if I phrased the substance of my first question differently, their reply would give me different clues, allowing me to solve the riddles of both their prophecies. It was certainly worth a try.

"*Where* shall I find my master, the great wizard Ebenezum?"

"Here is the answer!" the Two Fates shouted together.

"Ye shall ever higher go—" Victoria began.

There was a moment of silence.

"And then directions they will show!" Mary Jane concluded triumphantly.

The Fates glanced at each other.

"Doesn't work much better, does it?" Victoria admitted.

Mary Jane nodded. "That bit missing in the middle does seem important."

"Still," Victoria volunteered, "go and show have a lot better rhymes than shibboleth. Blow, flow, snow—"

"Flambeau, undertow, outgrow—" Mary Jane added helpfully.

"Mistletoe, overthrow—" Victoria mentioned. "Why, the possibilities are virtually endless!" But her enthusiasm deflated almost immediately. "Oh, dear, that could be even more of a problem, couldn't it?"

"Indeed—" I began.

"No, no!" Victoria interrupted. "There's no need for you to even mention it! These prophecies of ours do tend to build. I'll move over to the central pillar of my own accord. That way, next time you ask a question, you'll get the most important part of our foretelling!"

The fate stepped over to the next pedestal. "It's too bad about Hortense. I don't suppose any of you have any prediction experience? No, you don't look like the type."

"It is a shame," Mary Jane added. "If only we had something or someone to fill in on the third platform. Even a crystal ball would do!"

I felt a sudden urge to clear my throat.

"Indeed," Snarks remarked.

The fates looked at me with concern. "You'd better watch out there," Victoria cautioned. "It's very easy to catch cold in the mountain air."

I assured the Fates that I was as well as could be expected under the circumstances. Perhaps, I suggested, it was time to get on with the prophecies.

"Very well," Victoria replied. "Now we shall answer one question—no more, no less. Ask mortal, and let the Fates reply!"

"Indeed," I said for what—I must admit—I was glad was the final time. I had gotten nowhere asking about my master. Perhaps, then, I should ask about my other pressing concern, and hope there was something—anything—in the answer that I might find useful. I spoke again:

"How might I defeat Death, and keep him from taking me prisoner?"

"Here is the answer!" the Two Fates cried with finality. There was a moment of silence.

"You will do just as you please," Victoria announced.

"And manage all of Death's decrees!" Mary Jane concluded.

"That was even worse than the other ones!" Snarks exclaimed.

"Oh, come on, now," Hubert chided the demon. "Give them credit. It's always hard when you break up an act. And yet they go on with the show! What troopers!"

"No," Mary Jane interjected. "The small obnoxious fellow was right. If anything, that prophecy was even more incomplete than the first two."

Victoria looked uncomfortably at her sister fate. "Well, maybe we can come up with something. It is their last prophecy, after all. What rhymes with please and decrees?"

"Almost everything," Mary Jane replied miserably.

"Well," Victoria admitted, "we've never done this before, but maybe, if we really, *really* try, we can eke out some glimmer of that first third of the riddle."

"It's worth a try," Mary Jane agreed. "They did come a long way, after all, with no idea that Hortense would be off somewhere gallivanting about when they arrived. Let's see, what do we have so far?"

"—you will do just as you please, and manage all of Death's decrees!" Victoria replied.

"Exactly!" Mary Jane paused to ponder. "I've heard that sort of prophecy before. It's one of those where the first line usually begins with 'if.'"

"Almost always!" Victoria cheered. "Actually, those prophecies usually begin with a phrase: 'If you should—'"

"That's right!" Mary Jane smiled out at me. "See,

we're halfway there already. If you should—uh—da da da da da. Well, it's certainly worth a try."

"I should say so!" Victoria replied. "Both of us will close our eyes and say whatever comes into our heads."

"With luck," Mary Jane added, "one of them will be the prophecy." She turned to her fellow fate. "Are you ready?"

"Whenever you are."

The two fates closed their eyes and swayed back and forth upon their pedestals.

Victoria spoke first:

"If you should shout cacophonies?"

Mary Jane answered a moment later:

"If you should tap him on the knees?"

Victoria moaned and spoke again:

"If you should do a full striptease?"

"If you should eat some cottage cheese?" Mary Jane added immediately.

Both fates opened their eyes and made more or less the same horrible sequence of faces.

"That was pretty terrible," Victoria allowed.

Mary Jane agreed. "When the muse leaves me, I'm worthless."

I thanked them both, and said that it was time we took our leave. My master was in dire distress in the land of Death, and for all I knew that danger might be growing with every passing minute. We would have to try and contact Plaugg, and rely on his ever so slightly godlike powers to come to our aid.

"Bless his minimal resplendence," Snarks added reverentially.

In the meantime, I added, I would consider their prophecies, and surely find some helpful clues therein.

It was only then that I remembered.

"Oh, no!" I exclaimed. In my concern for my master, I had completely forgotten to ask them the directions to heaven. I sheepishly explained my omission.

"Oh, dear," Mary Jane replied.

"Quite a shame," Victoria added.

"Do you think it would have done you any good, anyway?" Snarks demanded. "Do you understand anything these two have told you?"

"If only we could—" Mary Jane began.

"Now, now," Victoria reprimanded. "You know the rules. Three questions—"

"—no more, no less," Mary Jane agreed miserably.

"And they've all been used up," Victoria concluded. "However, that's in our official role. Perhaps we might be able to advise them unofficially?"

I looked hopefully at the two immortals. Could they actually help us, after all, even after my bumbling mistake?

"Oh, do you think we might?" Mary Jane asked, a bit of cheer returned to her voice.

"Oh, why not?" Victoria replied. "It's the least we can do with Hortense gone. Listen, mortals, to what the Fates suggest." She pointed above her. "Heaven, to the best of our knowledge, is somewhere up there."

"Up," Mary Jane agreed. "Definitely up."

"Exactly *where* up there I'm afraid we're a little vague on," Victoria added.

"They never invite us to any of their parties," Mary Jane explained.

"Yes," Victoria sighed. "Something like that would certainly brighten up a Saturday night!"

"Well, never mind about our social lives—if you could call them that," Mary Jane hastily amended. "Rather, shall we say—" She glanced at her sister.

The Two Fates smiled as one. "We hope we've helped you with your quest."

I thanked the immortal sisters and we took our leave, passing back through the portal and back to the mountainside, the Fates' final words carried to us through the thin, high air:

"I do wish Hortense would send us a card!"

"Well, that was certainly educational," Snarks remarked when we had gotten some distance from the temple. "I now know where not to come when I'm looking for answers."

" 'Twas nobody's fault," I amended. " 'Tis but one more difficulty on our road."

"Our road is nothing but difficulties!" Snarks complained.

"Indeed," Hubert the dragon rumbled. "And because this journey failed, I now have another difficulty which I cannot avoid."

"What do you mean?" I asked the morose-looking reptile.

Hubert sighed mightily, his nostrils emitting a prodigious amount of steam. "I must go somewhere where I swore I would never go again. But it is a place where we will surely get the answers to your questions. I must do it, for since I have met you and the wizard, that meeting has opened up my life. I owe the wizard this journey out of gratitude. Let us hope I survive the experience. If you would climb on my back?"

Snarks and I did as Hubert bade.

"Hang on!" the dragon announced. And we were airborne once again.

NINE

When pleading for your life with demons, dragons, or the various monsters one encounters within the sorcerous arts, it is generally not wise to place too much of the argument for the continuation of one's existence on the needs of one's family and other relations, for, let us face it, demons, dragons and various monsters also have families and other relations, and, thinking of their own maiden aunts and mothers-in-law, may eat you as an act of mercy.

—From *The Teachings of Ebenezum*,
Volume XLI.

"Indeed," I asked the dragon once we were safely aloft, "would it be too much trouble to tell us where you are taking us?"

"No, I suppose not," Hubert replied miserably. "I just want to get this over with." His scales shook beneath us. Had the giant reptile shivered?

"We'd like to get this over with, too!" Snarks exclaimed. "So tell us, already!"

"Very well," Hubert answered, gloom still pervading his tones. "We have to go to the home of the dragons."

"Indeed?" I said, somewhat surprised.

"That's it?" Snarks stated rather more baldly. "What's wrong with that?"

"Plenty, I assure you," the dragon continued morosely. "But it's worse than that." Hubert sighed. "We have to go see Morty."

"Morty?" Snarks asked.

"Is there a problem with Morty?" I suggested.

"Is there a problem?" Hubert shot forth a plume of fire. "How can I make you, who are not dragons, and not subject to the dictates of strict dragon society—how can I *possibly* make you understand?"

"Indeed," I gently prompted. "I imagine we have already been together far longer, and gotten to know each other far better, than any human, demon and dragon ever have before! Why not tell us your problem, and we will attempt to comprehend?"

"Yes, why not?" the dragon agreed not too enthusiastically. "It will at least help pass the time until we get"—he shivered again—"there."

Hubert paused, billows of smoke cascading from his nostrils. I held my breath as the fumes passed me by, fearful that if I coughed I might break the reptile's concentration.

"Where can I begin?" Hubert began.

"This is going to be long-winded, isn't it?" Snarks whispered fatalistically.

"I guess you could say I've always been a different sort of dragon," Hubert continued, already swept up in the drama of his narrative. "Not that I wasn't given plenty of chances to fit in. I could have gone into one of the acceptable dragon occupations: world conquest, gold hoarding, damsel-napping, distant and ethereal flight patterns. But no, I had to strike out on my own. The theater had found its way into my ice-cold reptile blood!

"You see, it all started in my apprenticeship days. One of the older dragons—my Uncle Spike, actually—had taken me down to the world of men for some of my elementary lessons—uh, Panic and Mayhem 101, I believe. So here I was, supposed to stomp and snort and scare the population

into fleeing willy-nilly—that was the general purpose of
the lesson, you see. But my uncle had made the mistake of
setting us down in the middle of this large community on
market day.

"Uncle Spike then went off to scare a few humans in
my direction; you know, to get the ball rolling, as it were.
But he had unwittingly left me in a spot that would change
my very life!" The dragon emitted a long, nostalgic sigh.
"For, not fifty yards distant from where I landed, stood a
Punch and Judy show!"

"A Punch and Judy show?" Snarks commented. "Sounds
pretty impressive to me!"

"Yes," Hubert replied happily, too far lost in memory
to note the demon's sarcasm. "Punch and Judy and all the
rest. How I loved those little puppets!"

"This isn't only going to be long-winded," Snarks
despaired. "This is going to be maudlin!"

Hubert laughed a sad little laugh. "Oh, I was lost within
a minute of setting my eyes on that tiny stage. You see,
there was not only a Punch puppet, and a Judy puppet, and
a policeman puppet—there was a dragon puppet, too!"

"Oh, that explains everything!" Snarks remarked.

I thought of cautioning the demon to silence, but Hubert
was oblivious to all but the story of his life.

"Yes," the dragon continued. "There it was, before
me, all of life on that tiny stage. Punch hit Judy, Judy hit
Punch, the policeman hit both of them, they hit the policeman back. Then the dragon came in, and things got *really*
interesting!"

Hubert stopped talking suddenly. I looked past his head
and saw we were approaching another distant mountain.

"Oh, dear," the dragon moaned.

This, I guessed, was Hubert's ancestral home.

We flew on through the clouds, and I got a better look
at our destination. It was not your typical mountain. Oh, it
was high enough, and it had crags and rocky outcroppings
to spare. But it was totally lacking a peak. What should be
the final quarter or so of the mountain (if it had followed
the rules generally used for this sort of thing) was missing,

replaced instead by a broad plateau; a space, I realized as we approached, of some size.

"The home of the dragons," Hubert noted morosely, his enthusiasm fled. We neared our destination with excruciating slowness. Had Hubert deliberately reduced his speed?

"Indeed," I said. Obviously, the dragon did not look forward to this homecoming. I had a feeling he might be overdramatizing his problems. But then, I have never visited the home of the dragons. Perhaps, I thought, it was best to get Hubert's mind off of what was to come. And I could think of but one way to do this.

"Hubert," I reminded him gently, "you never finished telling us your story."

"What?" the dragon asked, his moping temporarily disturbed. "Oh, you mean about that town and Uncle Spike and Punch and Judy. All that?"

"That's all right," Snarks reassured him. "You don't *have* to tell us."

"No, no," Hubert insisted. "What's the use of starting a story if you're not willing to get to the point? It's not fair to your audience!"

"Indeed," I interjected before the demon could comment further. "So why don't you finish?"

Hubert nodded grimly. "The show must go on, even if I do have to see Morty. Now, where was I? Oh, that's right. Punch and Judy, and then the dragon puppet. Well, let me tell you, I was lost! Uncle Spike kept sending harried villagers my way, and I didn't fry a single one of them! I didn't even know they were there! I didn't pay any attention to the audience of the puppet show, either, though I vaguely remember some children screaming and fleeing in panic. I was totally absorbed in the action on the tiny stage—Punch hit the dragon, Judy hit the dragon, the dragon hit Judy, the dragon hit Punch. And then the policeman showed up!"

"You did have to encourage him, didn't you?" Snarks muttered.

"I don't need to tell you, I was excited. Here was the Punch and Judy show, with all the audience and miscella-

neous other citizenry fled. It was a show performed only
for me! And I began to think, if an audience applauded a
dragon puppet, then consider what their reaction to the
real thing would be!''

"Indeed," I agreed. " 'Tis a thought to ponder."

"Rather than talk about," Snarks added, "especially at
great length."

"Well," I stated, "it certainly was an inspirational
story."

"Unfortunately," Hubert admitted, "it was more flam-
mable than inspirational. As I became more involved in
the puppet show, I waddled closer and closer to that tiny
stage. Then the puppet dragon got the upper hand!'' Hubert coughed delicately. "At that tender age, you don't
have quite the control over your flame that you might. In
my enthusiasm, I'm afraid I burned the booth to the ground.
The puppeteer got away unharmed, but I fear I singed
Punch and Judy beyond recognition. Which was fortunate,
because, when Uncle Spike arrived, I could at least show
him a little mayhem."

"Did he buy it?" Snarks asked, interested despite himself.

"I got a passing grade," Hubert acknowledged. "But
my exams no longer mattered. From that moment onward I
had but one goal—the theater!"

The dragon sighed. "But that doesn't matter anymore.
In a few minutes, we will be—*there* again!"

"But can it be that bad?" I asked.

"That bad," Hubert agreed miserably. "And worse!
Dragons will never appreciate show business!"

"At last, someone I can relate to," Snarks stated with
new enthusiasm. "Sounds like dragons are my kind of
creature!"

"They are if you like burning and conquering and de-
vouring and hoarding," Hubert said glumly. "Dragons are
very good at that!" He blew a despairing puff of smoke.
"Hubert—they'd ask me—Hubert, don't you like to rend
and tear and destroy? Don't you like amassing gold? You
want to do what? Act? But aren't burning and destroying
and hoarding all acts? Oh, they would never understand.
And Morty!''

"Morty?" Snarks asked.

"Yes, Morty was always the worst—my older brother, excelling at all those things for which I had no aptitude—basic mayhem, applied burning, advanced treasure collection—he passed them all with honors!"

"Morty?" Snarks said again.

"And now I have to go back and face all that one more time!" Hubert concluded.

"Indeed," I said reassuringly. "Perhaps it will not be as bad as you imagine."

But Hubert laughed bitterly. "Oh, no. It will be as bad as that and worse. Believe me, you do not know the depths that dragons will sink to! But I will be strong, for your master! I will persevere, for your master. I will even see Morty, for your master. And we will find the way to heaven, after all!"

"Morty?" Snarks interjected again.

"We are almost there," Hubert remarked. "I'm going to angle in for a landing. Hang on! And once we get there, let me do the talking."

"Must we?" Snarks asked, his words almost lost to the increasing wind. But then he and I both were forced to lean down against the reptile and clutch his scales.

Hubert landed smoothly in a clearing on the edge of the plateau. A single, dark gray dragon, almost indistinguishable from the surrounding rock, watched our descent.

Hubert came to a full stop and looked at the other reptile. "I think I know that dragon."

"I can't hear you!" the other dragon called. "I have carrots in my ears!"

"I beg your pardon?" Hubert replied.

"It is you, isn't it?" the other dragon cheered. "You wouldn't know about this, would you? You've been away. Well, I can tell you, nephew, it's all your fault!"

"Oh, dear," Hubert whispered. "It's my Uncle Spike."

"Nice to see you again!" Uncle Spike continued as he trotted towards us. "We've heard how well you've been doing down below. You can't imagine the furor that's caused!" The dragon chuckled, sending sparks flying out from between his teeth. "And what's that on your back? A gift or two for your Uncle Spike? Perhaps a few munchies?"

"Certainly not!" Hubert said hastily. "These are my companions on a very important quest. I'm afraid I didn't have time to bring gifts, uncle. This is not a pleasure visit, but rather a necessary stop on a mission that could change the course of destiny!"

"Ah, nephew, it's easy to see how you can wow them down on the surface world. What a sense of style!"

"Thank you, I'm sure," Hubert replied softly, taken aback by the compliment. "I never expected to hear something like that in the land of the dragons."

"A lot has changed around here," Spike agreed. "And it's all because of you!"

"Maybe," Snarks piped up hopefully, "they've outlawed musical comedy."

"Oho!" Uncle Spike cried, looking at the demon for the first time. "Who is this tidbit?"

"Are you demeaning my size?" Snarks demanded. "I am a full-grown demon!"

"Oh, dear, no," Spike replied with a shake of his massive head. "On the contrary, I am complimenting your taste."

"Really?" Snarks responded, surprised. He self-consciously fingered his heavy woolen attire. "Oh, it's nothing, really. These are just some old robes from my religious order."

"Oh, no, no," Spike chided. "You misunderstand. Not taste as in selection of wardrobe. More like taste as in the opportunity to become a light snack. And may I say, you certainly look yummy!"

"I'm sorry," Snarks replied. "I was supposed to let Hubert do the talking."

"Yes, uncle," Hubert interjected. "These two on my back are under my protection. They are crucial to the completion of my task. I would appreciate it, therefore, if you would stop considering them as light meals."

"Oho!" Spike guffawed. "That's a good one! Under an actor's protection?" Flame shot twenty feet in the air as he roared with laughter. "Wait until I tell the others about that one! I tell you, Hubert, you can certainly see that you're a professional!"

"I suppose so, uncle," Hubert replied doubtfully. "But, enjoyable as it is to talk to you, I'm afraid we have a mission to complete. I therefore must see my brother Morty as quickly as possible."

"Morty?" Spike responded, still amused. "His horde is just over here in the next crag. You haven't been here in a while, have you? Well, I'll be glad to show you the way." He looked speculatively at Snarks and myself. "A reptile can certainly get hungry this time of day, it being between meals and all. I could really stand a little pick-me-up. Do you really need two—"

"Yes, Uncle Spike," Hubert replied firmly.

"Simply asking! No need to get upset." Spike's tongue darted from his mouth to taste the air in our vicinity. "And let me know if you change your mind."

"Morty, Uncle Spike?"

"Surely," the large reptile nodded as he turned to lead the way. "I'm simply putting in my request now, before all the other dragons see your tasty—um—companions. Remember, my boy, you should always spare a kindly thought for your elders."

Spike walked toward the interior of the plateau, and Hubert followed.

"Indeed," I whispered to the latter dragon as we strode across the barren rock. "Is this what you were so worried about?"

"Yes and no," Hubert whispered back. "Uncle Spike has been more pleasant than I ever thought he could be. But there is something strange going on here."

"You mean his constant desire to eat us?" I suggested.

"No, no," Hubert disagreed. "That's perfectly natural for a dragon. I meant some of the comments he's been making. 'I can't hear you—I have carrots in my ears?' There seem to have been some fundamental changes in dragon society."

"But couldn't that be for the good?" I reasoned.

"Nothing in dragon society is ever for the good," Hubert replied morosely. "I am more worried now than I was before we came here."

"Great," Snarks replied. "Well, it's been nice knowing you. Or at least as nice as it can be knowing a human and a dragon."

If I had been surprised by the fatalism of Snarks's remark, I was even more surprised when Hubert nodded his agreement.

"It will get worse. We still have to see Morty."

TEN

Q: Are dragons hungry?
A: Is the sky blue?
Q: Are dragons fast?
A: Should a tax collector be avoided whenever possible?
Q: Do dragons eat wizards?
A: Have you forgotten to remind the reptiles of your facility with indigestion spells?

—From *Ask Mr. Magic:*
A Wizard's Guide to 364 of Today's Most Pressing Sorcerous Problems, scholastic edition,
by Ebenezum,
greatest wizard in the Western Kingdoms

Uncle Spike led us to the entrance of a very large cave.

"This is the place," the older dragon chuckled. "Allow me to introduce us." He yelled into the cave:

"Let your pages do the walking through the yellow fingers!"

"It's no wonder, with prices like that!" another voice roared in response.

Spike and the voice inside the cave laughed heartily.

"I'm beginning to see a pattern here," Hubert muttered darkly. "A pattern I don't like at all."

91

"Come on," Spike waved for us to follow. "Let's go in and see Morty."

"Morty?" Snarks, obviously unable to help himself, said again.

Hubert reluctantly followed.

"Hey, Morty!" Spike called. "Guess who's here? It's your brother Huey!"

"Huey?" Snarks asked.

"I told you I didn't want to come back here," Hubert replied.

"What?" Morty's voice called. "The smokeless wonder is back again? Well, come on in!"

"I suppose I have to," Hubert murmured, walking forward as if every step was an effort.

"The smokeless won—" Snarks began before a particularly sharp look from me silenced him. I figured that Hubert was in enough distress without a demonic chorus.

The dragon carried us into a truly massive cavern, larger even than the great hall at the wizards' college. But what really took my breath away were the huge tapestries covering every available foot of walls and ceiling, each great hanging sporting a sewn-in message.

SEE THE SOUTHERN KINGDOMS!
MOTHER DUCK'S REALM—A FAIRYLAND
FOR MERE PIECES OF GOLD!
THE WESTERN KINGDOMS—THERE'S MORE
THERE THAN MEETS THE EYE!
THE LAND OF THE DRAGONS—YOUR VACATION
IN THE CLOUDS!

Each of the tapestries also featured elaborate illustrations. The one concerning the Southern Kingdoms showed a large picture of the sun, while the Mother Duck hanging prominently displayed a large castle. Only the tapestry for the Western Kingdoms was fairly nondescript.

And in the midst of the tapestries squatted the largest dragon I had ever seen, half again the size of Hubert and bright red besides.

"Huey!" the huge reptile rumbled. "And how's my pip-squeak brother?"

"I'm glad to see you, too, Morty," Hubert managed miserably.

"Hear you've done pretty well down among the humans," Morty went on cheerily. "Who would've thought it?"

"Morty," Hubert said, barely managing his temper, "I'm here for a reason."

"Really?" his brother remarked heartily. "You want another flame-shooting contest? Or maybe we can compare our gold hordes?"

"It's no time for games, Morty," Hubert replied. "Besides, you always win."

"And you always were a spoilsport, Huey," Morty chuckled. "But maybe I can do something for you, anyway."

"I understand you've got a successful travel business—" Hubert continued doggedly.

"You see it all around you!" Morty cheered, tossing his massive head back and forth at the various tapestries that crowded the room. "At last, I've found a way to satisfy a dragon's wanderlust! Yes, you could say Morty's Travel is a roaring success. What else would you expect from your older brother? But you said you needed help."

There was a commotion at the mouth of the cave.

"That was no lady," a voice called, "that was my wife!"

"The joke's on him," another voice added. "The mouse is a ventriloquist."

"Sorry," Morty yelled back. "You can't get in here without a tie!"

Morty and Spike laughed along with the two new voices. Hubert shivered quietly.

"My worst fears have been realized," he whispered.

The floor shook as two other dragons, one a dull orange, the other sort of a red-brick tone, trundled into the back of the cave.

"Dewey!" Morty greeted the newcomers. "Ferdie!"

"Dewey?" Snarks repeated. "Ferdie?"

"Oh, my," the dull-orange dragon remarked as he glanced our way. "Hors-devours."

"I've done it again, haven't I?" Snarks whispered in horror. I nodded. The demon did have a way of attracting the attention of others. Very large others. It was interesting, I reflected, how ineffectual one seemed in the presence of giant reptiles. I might have a magic sword and a magic ferret, but what use was either of them against fire-breathing lizards? I thought again of the Brownie, but realized that even shoe magic would be ineffectual against creatures of this size; creatures who seemed to be showing all too much interest in Snarks and me.

"No, no, Ferdie!" Hubert interjected. "These are friends."

"Very appetizing friends," Ferdie agreed. "But we shouldn't eat before we are properly introduced, should we?"

"Always know your food," Dewey agreed. "That's a dragon's guide to happy digestion."

"So!" Morty boomed. "What brings you fellows here? Need a few travel tips?"

"We always get our travel tips from you," Ferdie said.

"Wouldn't go anyplace else than Morty's Travel," Dewey amplified.

"That's why we're number one!" Morty exclaimed cheerily. "Of course, with me in charge, what else could we be?"

"Still, there are improvements that could be made," Ferdie continued, eyeing Snarks and me with far too much interest.

"Most certainly," Dewey added, saliva dripping from his huge incisors. "Like the introduction of a snack tray for hungry customers."

"Yes!" Uncle Spike agreed from the far side of the room. "The very idea that I suggested earlier!"

"It doesn't have to be anything out of the ordinary," Dewey explained further. "Simply some of your dragon staples. Say, like these fellows here. Nice, bite-size creatures from down below. So round, so soft, so succulent!"

"Yes, soft is a must," Ferdie concurred. "None of

those exotic things with exoskeletons, please! They hurt my teeth."

"Never eat an unknown species," Spike added sagely.

"Another tip for happy dragon digestion," Dewey concluded. "But how do we split them up?"

"They are a little on the small side," Ferdie agreed.

"Oh, everyone will get their share," Uncle Spike assured them. "Anybody got a knife?"

"Wait a second!" Hubert roared. "Hasn't anybody been listening? My friends are not for eating!"

"Not even a bite?" Ferdie frowned.

"Look at all the arms and legs they have," Dewey demanded. "Surely they wouldn't miss one or two?"

"Out of the question!" Hubert replied adamantly.

"Huey never was one to share his playthings," Morty remarked.

"Share them?" Hubert retorted. "If you saw them, you took them!"

"Now, now, boys," Uncle Spike chided. "We shouldn't let old family grudges spoil this fine reunion, should we? Let's put all thoughts of eating and generously sharing our food aside for a moment, and officially welcome Hubert back to his homeland!"

Dewey and Ferdie cheered.

"So you really are a song-and-dance dragon?" Ferdie asked enthusiastically.

"We've got all your clippings," Dewey added. "At least all of those we could find on our trips through the lowlands."

"It's sort of a sideline while we're pillaging and burning," Ferdie explained.

"Yes, yes," Morty interrupted. "I'm sure we're all glad to see Huey again. But isn't it time to talk travel?"

"That's right," Dewey harmonized. "We always come to Morty's travel. After all, isn't Morty Hubert's brother?"

"His brother? B-but that's beside the point when Morty's gives you such great travel services!" Morty insisted.

"Yes," Ferdie appended. "We figured if we came here often enough, we were bound to meet the famous member of the family."

"*Another* side benefit of Morty's Travel!" the large red dragon stressed. "Although a very minor one."

"Of course, when we were waiting around for you to show, we had to do some business with Morty," Dewey elucidated. "I tell you, being a fan can be so expensive!"

"So what business do you want to do *now*?" Morty emphasized. "We have deals you wouldn't believe!"

"I'm sure you do," Ferdie replied. "But for the moment, we would like to talk to your brother."

"Yes," Dewey enthused. "You must tell us all about your experiences on the stage!"

"You really want to know about my experiences?" Hubert answered in disbelief.

"These deals won't last forever!" Morty ventured. No one seemed to notice.

"Are you kidding?" Spike laughed. "Every dragon here wants to know about your experiences. Your success has had a profound effect upon the entirety of dragon culture!"

"So that's what that was all about!" Hubert marveled.

"These offers are for a limited time only!" Morty remarked rather more loudly than was necessary. He was ignored by the others.

"The punch lines," Hubert went on. "When I heard you exchange them, I was afraid you were mocking everything I stood for."

"The punch lines?" Snarks asked.

"Quiet, appetizers," Dewey admonished. "We'll deal with you presently."

Snarks quieted.

"On the contrary—" Ferdie began. "You should consider the custom an honor—"

"Mockery was the furthest thing from our minds," Dewey further assured. "When we heard of your success telling jokes, it opened up whole new vistas for dragonkind."

"That's right!" Uncle Spike agreed. "And soon we all began to tell jokes!"

"As a way of greeting—" Ferdie added.

"It became the 'in' thing to do—" Dewey expounded.

"This could be," Morty cried hoarsely, "a once-in-a-lifetime opportunity!'' The others continued talking as if he wasn't even there.

"Of course, telling a complete joke every time you greet someone can be very time-consuming,'' Spike maintained.

"So, over time, we shortened the form,'' Ferdie clarified.

"I see,'' the dragon upon which we sat interposed. "And now you simply say the best part, like—'' Hubert paused.

"Oh, oh,'' Ferdie hollered. "Would you—could you—if it wouldn't be asking too much—do a punch line?''

"Yes, yes,'' Dewey huzzahed. "Do one for us, Huey. Please?''

"Oh, very well. If I must.'' Hubert considered for a moment, before speaking again:

"Because his pink ones were in the wash.''

All the dragons save Morty guffawed heartily.

"He's already a master!'' Dewey marveled.

"Why hadn't we seen his genius before?'' Ferdie queried.

"You may *never* see bargains like this again!'' Morty screamed. No one even bothered to glance at him.

"Well, we certainly see it now,'' Uncle Spike asserted. "Huey, you will have to tell us all your secrets.''

"Secrets?'' Hubert responded doubtfully.

"Yes,'' Ferdie explicated, "you know, how you entice humans and others into seeing your act.''

"How?'' Hubert ruminated. "Well, you know, publicity, word of mouth. . . .''

"I'm sure we'll learn about the preparation soon enough,'' Dewey chirruped. "We want to hear how you put audiences under your reptile spell!''

"Really?'' Hubert responded dubiously. "Well, I guess you could call it that. I do have a partner, you know. We start out with a little song, a little dance, then really hook them with some snappy patter.''

"And then you eat them!'' Uncle Spike suggested.

"Pardon?'' Hubert replied, somewhat aghast.

"I thought that would naturally be what happens next,'' Spike expounded.

"Most certainly not!'' Hubert contradicted. "Once you

have the audience with you, you milk their emotions for all it's worth. You know, a sensitive song of lost love, followed by a specialty dance number and a rousing, patriotic finale!''

"Oh, I see," Spike answered with sudden comprehension. "And *then* you eat them!"

"Uh"—Hubert hesitated—"no. Then it's time for the audience to applaud wildly, so that you can come back for your encore."

"Obviously," Ferdie interjected, "we don't understand any of the finer points of your newly chosen profession."

"Quite right," Dewey assented. "But tell us, Huey old dragon. When exactly *do* you eat them?"

"Oh, my." Hubert looked at the others. "I'm afraid I don't."

"You don't eat them?" Spike erupted incredulously.

"You don't eat *anybody*?" Ferdie echoed.

"It all seems rather pointless, doesn't it?" Dewey agreed with the others. "How do you survive?"

"Well," Hubert replied a bit defensively, "I do get paid a bit."

"Paid?" Uncle Spike chuckled. "You sly reptile!"

"What a horde of gold you must have!" Ferdie marveled.

The other dragons—save Morty, who was sulking in a corner—all smoked heartily.

"Well, it's been quite nice to visit with all of you again," Hubert puffed. "But I must speak with my brother."

The red dragon in the corner raised his head.

"Morty's the one to go to for travel," Dewey agreed.

"Of course," Ferdie interjected, "we can travel anytime. But it's not every day we get to talk to a star!"

"Thanks again," Hubert replied modestly. "But if I might be able to talk to my brother alone?"

"Fair enough," Spike piped up as he eyed Snarks and me speculatively. "Would you like me to watch your snacks?"

"Oh second thought," Hubert amended hastily, "I believe it would be in everybody's interest if my two companions also consulted with Morty."

"Doesn't sound very interesting to me," Spike remarked.

He glanced at Dewey and Ferdie. "What do you fellows think?"

"We'll do anything," Ferdie enthused, "if you'll put on a show!"

"Well, I don't know—" Hubert hesitated.

"No show, no go!" Ferdie insisted.

"And, you know," Dewey added ominously as he breathed a thin line of smoke in our direction, "all this talking has made me hungry."

"Oh, all right!" Hubert relented. "I'll do a show. But just a little one!"

Dewey and Ferdie both applauded.

"We knew we could twist your tail!" Dewey exclaimed.

"We'll have to go out and tell the others!" Ferdie added.

"Yep," Uncle Spike agreed. "I'll have to get out of here right now to tell your Aunt Louise."

"Louise?" Snarks piped up before his demon hands covered his mouth.

"My, this one certainly is a talkative tidbit," Spike remarked, moving his smoking snout rather closer to us than was comfortable.

"Now, uncle," Hubert cautioned.

"Oh, we understand, Huey," Spike assured him. "There's no reason to be ashamed. I'm sure a traveler like you never knows where he might spend the night. It's always wise to bring an extra food supply."

"In fact," Dewey added, "it's a cornerstone of dragon digestion."

"Life on the road must certainly be tough," Ferdie continued. "Far be it from us to force you to share what might be your only sustenance."

"But—" Hubert responded.

"Say no more," Spike interrupted. "We understand. But maybe, after the performance, we can trade you a real meal for those tidbits!"

"But—" Hubert tried again.

"No need to thank us!" Ferdie assured him.

"But—" Hubert insisted.

"We have to go tell the others about the show!" Dewey called as he left with Ferdie and Spike.

"But—" Hubert began again. But the three dragons were gone.

"Oh, dear," Snarks whispered.

"Indeed," I agreed. "We will have to be careful in our dealings with dragons. Otherwise, we will end our days as somebody's lunch."

Hubert sighed. " 'Tis the nature of dragons. They always look at the world through their stomachs."

" 'Tis rather the nature of an adventurous life," I assured the dragon. "I have been threatened with digestion by many other species in the course of my travels. It's the sort of thing you come to count on in the apprenticeship business."

"I suppose you're going to say it's my fault that the dragons noticed us so much," Snarks said defensively. "And I suppose it is."

The demon groaned. "There's something about dragon names," Snarks despaired. "I can't help myself."

"Oh, well," Hubert allowed. "I can understand that with Spike."

"You can?" Snarks replied uncomprehendingly.

"Certainly," the dragon explained. " 'Spike' is only my uncle's nickname. His real name is Bruce."

"Bruce?" Snarks repeated, unable to do otherwise.

"I agree entirely," Hubert consented. "What kind of name is that for a dragon?"

He looked over at his brother, who still moped in the corner. "But I must speak with Morty if we are to complete our mission."

Morty straightened as we approached. "And what do *you* want?"

"I need your help," Hubert explained. "That's why I'm here."

"You need *my* help?" Morty ventured incredulously. "Hubert, the star, condescends to ask something from his humble travel-agent brother, so lowly a dragon that others only use his services because of his famous relations?"

"He's taking this a little hard, isn't he?" Snarks commented.

"Drama runs in the family," Hubert explained.

It seemed to me that this drama had run far enough. Now that we were not in immediate danger of being eaten for a chance remark, perhaps there was something I could do to remedy this situation.

"Indeed," I interjected. "And I am sure he would be very good at it, had he chosen drama as his profession. In fact, he might have been even better than you, Hubert."

The other dragon's ears perked up. "I might?"

"Certainly," I hurriedly added. "But he chose an even more noble dragon profession, that of guiding his fellows through the skies!"

"I did?" Morty replied. He took a moment to dust off his wings. "I did!"

"I see what you're saying," Hubert continued, picking up on my cue. "Look, Morty, what does it matter what others think? We know who's the older brother around here, don't we?"

"Yes," Morty said uncertainly, "I guess that hasn't changed." He absently flexed his wing muscles. "Want to try a little flying contest?"

"Why bother?" Hubert conceded. "We both know you'd win. Plus, we don't have much time. We need your help now."

Morty snorted a tentative bit of smoke. "Oh, well, if you put it that way, I suppose we could work out something, if only because you're my brother."

"Morty, I knew I could count on you!" Hubert enthused. "Now, can you tell me the way to heaven?"

"Heaven?" Morty frowned. "I always thought it was— you know—up." He looked distractedly about the room. "But maybe I can find better directions."

He strolled over to the Western Kingdoms tapestry. "I keep all my odd maps and information back here. So few dragons want to go to the Western Kingdoms—such a dreary place!—that I have plenty of room." He sat back on his haunches and pushed the tapestry aside with his snout.

"Let's see," he ruminated. "Ah. The very file." He ruffled through a pile of parchment. "This could be a bit of a problem. Heaven appears to be awfully large."

"Indeed!" I called helpfully. "We seek the whereabouts of a minor deity, a Plaugg?"

"The inconsequentially majestic!" Snarks added.

"Ah." Morty nodded, brightening considerably. "The lowest level possible, huh? Well, that should make things a little easier." He pulled a piece of parchment from the bottom of the pile. "Here we go." He handed the document to Hubert. "You have to travel up, and a little to the left."

Hubert glanced over the directions. "Seems simple enough."

"Of course it is!" the other dragon insisted. "Morty's Travel has the best directions available!"

"This should do nicely," Hubert agreed. "What do we owe you?"

Morty considered. "Well, you do have those two succulent—but no, you want to hold on to them for some reason. Let us just say that I should be happiest when you're gone. I ask, therefore, for your speediest exit possible."

"Then, brother, I am gone," Hubert assured him, backing out of the cave with his two passengers still intact.

"Oh, no, you're not!" Dewey and Ferdie echoed from the cave mouth. "It's showtime!"

ELEVEN

"There is no business like show business. There is also no business like certified public accounting, but that doesn't rhyme as well."

—From *Wake Up and Conjure:
A Wizard's Guide to Everyday Life,* fourth edition,
by Ebenezum,
greatest wizard in the Western Kingdoms

"But—" Hubert began.

"The beer that made Mel Famey walk us!" Ferdie declared.

"I've come for the man who shot my paw!" Dewey added.

"No one's going to make a gosh darn canoe out of me!" Hubert replied after a moment's consideration.

The dragons laughed at some length.

"That's the spirit!" Ferdie said encouragingly.

"Nothing special," Hubert stated. "Just show biz in the blood."

"That's exactly what we're looking for!" Dewey trumpeted. "And we're all ready for you. Everybody's gathered back at the landing plateau!"

"That's awfully nice, fellows," Hubert began, "but—"

"And they're calling for you!" Ferdie cried.

"They are?" Hubert smiled. "Well, let's not keep them waiting!"

"But Hubert!" I whispered in the dragon's ear. Hadn't he promised his brother to leave quickly? And hadn't we wasted enough time here in our search for my master?

Hubert made a shushing sound as he walked to meet the other dragons.

"Oho," Ferdie pointed out. "So now the other tidbit is bothering you?"

"Yes, they do seem like such an annoyance," Dewey agreed. "I'm sure you'll feel much better once you're rid of them."

"But—" Hubert began.

"You've held out on us for long enough!" Dewey insisted. "It's time for a snack."

"It's time for escape," Snarks whispered in my ear.

But Hubert shook his head vehemently.

"No, it is not," our dragon allowed. "Not with these fellows."

I silently repressed a cheer. Hubert would not let us down!

"Why not?" Ferdie demanded.

"Give us one good reason!" Dewey chorused.

"Um. A good reason?" Hubert replied uncertainly.

"Dragon's dinner, here we come," Snarks whispered.

But Hubert brightened, shouting: "Because they're part of the show!"

"Part of the show?" the two reptiles said in unison, the disappointment plain upon their dragon faces.

"I guess we'll have to wait, then," Dewey spoke reluctantly.

"At least until after the performance," Ferdie agreed.

"Very good," Hubert remarked with the proper note of imperiousness. "Now stand aside, so that my assistants and I might prepare for the show."

The other dragons deferentially made way for Hubert and his retinue.

"In show business," Hubert explained when we had reached a sufficient distance from the others, "it sometimes pays to be difficult."

"If that's the case," Snarks rejoined, "you should be incredibly wealthy."

I ignored the demon's remark, for I had other things on my mind.

"Indeed," I asked Hubert, "we're now part of the performance?"

"Don't worry," the dragon assured me. "We'll fake it."

"Fake it?" Snarks replied miserably. "Maybe I should have been a dragon's dinner, after all."

"You may still have a chance," Hubert remarked, "if the performance doesn't go well."

"Indeed?" I asked somewhat reluctantly.

Hubert nodded. "Dragons, as a rule, do not constitute a forgiving audience." He reached up and took off his top hat. "But here. You need to learn your lines." He pulled two sheaves of parchment from inside the hat brim, and handed them to me. I passed one of the two on to Snarks.

"You actually keep your music in your hat?" the demon asked incredulously.

"What—" The dragon chuckled, twirling the hat back atop his head. "Do you think I wear this thing just for show?"

I looked down at the piece of parchment in my hands. It was a song about dragons, with stanzas clearly marked with a number 1, 2 or 3.

"I thought this was a particularly appropriate little ditty, with three parts, of course. I shall be number one—that part carries much of the weight of the song. Wuntvor shall be number two, and Snarks number three. Simply follow my lead, and everything shall be fine. Any questions?"

"Yeah," Snarks piped up. "Do we have to do this?"

"I am afraid so,' Hubert responded. "I am not a solo act. My numbers require a partner. In addition, we need an excuse to keep the two of you off my fellow dragons' dinner tables."

Snarks swallowed hard.

"So it's sing . . . or be eaten?"

"That's about it," the dragon replied. "What shall it be?"

"I'm thinking!" the demon answered. "I'm thinking!"

Then Hubert rounded a bend and there were dragons everywhere.

"People who live in grass houses shouldn't stow thrones!" a delicate pink reptile called.

"I wouldn't send a knight out on a dog like this!" a large blue-green lizard added.

"Well, you wouldn't eat a fine pig like that all at once!" a bright yellow dragon chimed in.

"So I bit him!" a very large bluish-purple dragon rumbled.

And so it went, a hundred dragons shouting a hundred punch lines all at once, so that all you could hear were occasional references to dogs, chickens and salesmen, followed quickly by an overwhelming wave of laughter, then silence.

All the dragons were waiting for Hubert's response.

The showdragon cleared his throat.

"How he got into my pajamas, I'll never know."

Well, if there had been a house there, he would have brought it down. As it was, the audience's laughter seemed to shake the whole plateau. But then the laughter died down as well, and more than a hundred dragons looked at us expectantly.

"Is it my imagination," Snarks whispered, "or do these guys look like they haven't eaten in a week?"

"Quick!" Hubert instructed us. "Get down on either side of me. It's showtime!"

"But—" Snarks began.

But it was already too late. Hubert was singing:

> "Dragons are different, dragons are swell,
> Dragons can burn you with their sense of smell!"

He glanced over at me. That meant it was my turn! I quickly sang the words of my stanza, trying to repeat the tune Hubert had begun:

> "Dragons are different, it's useful to know,
> 'Cause one can crush you with his little toe."

"Isn't this song going to give these guys ideas?" Snarks whispered.

"Your turn!" I whispered back.

Snarks looked out at the assembled dragons and froze.

"Dinnertime!" I added.

Snarks cleared his throat and sang:

> "Dragons are different, it can't be revoked;
> They prefer their dinners thoroughly smoked."

"All together now!" Hubert declared. Snarks and I did our best to join the dragon in the chorus:

> "They're kings of all reptiles;
> Their manners divine,
> 'Cause all these dragons—
> Why, they're friends of mine!"

Snarks glanced at me, the edge of hysteria in his whispered plea:

"Why do I get the eating lines?"

It was then I noticed that Ferdie and Dewey had positioned themselves on Snarks's side of the performance, and were in addition watching the demon with more than routine interest.

"Here we go again!" Hubert prompted the two of us. He sang:

> "Dragons are different, they like to fly
> And pillage and burn—they're not at all shy!"

The audience had begun to clap along. Hubert had picked a real crowd pleaser. But it was my turn:

> "Dragons are different, both young and old;
> They take what they want, as long as it's gold!"

The crowd kept the rhythm up, even though Snarks was late coming in again. I glanced at the demon.

"I can't say this!" he whispered back.

"Dinner—" Hubert whispered from overhead.
Snarks sang:

> "Dragons are different, you can be sure,
>   When it comes to eating, they're not demure!"

Dewey and Ferdie seemed to like those lines. They had started to drool.

"All together once again!" Hubert called down to us. It was time for the chorus:

> "They're some lucky lizards
>   With scales so sublime,
>   And all these dragons—
>   Why, they're friends of mine!"

Then Hubert started to dance. Both Snarks and I scurried away to give him room. He stomped up and down while flapping his wings and shooting great gouts of flame into the air. The crowd couldn't get enough of him.

It took him a full five minutes to slow down, winded at last. He looked down at the two of us.

"Take it—uh—partners!" he wheezed.

"Take it?" Snarks whispered hysterically. "Take it where?"

"I think Hubert wants us to dance," I suggested.

"No self-respecting demon—" Snarks noticed that Ferdie and Dewey were leaning closer still.

The demon danced. My way, as I was dancing his way. Our feet managed to land in the same place at the same time. We tripped and fell. I tried to roll over and rise, but had somehow gotten my arms and scabbard stuck amidst the demon's robes. It took us a full minute to extricate ourselves from our predicament. We turned to face the crowd.

The audience loved it.

"What now?" Snarks whispered. "I don't have another food verse, do I?"

"The final chorus!" Hubert called. He and I sang while Snarks backed away from certain overzealous members of the audience.

"So call up a dragon
  If you want to dine;
  And all these dragons—
  Why, they're friends of mine!"

Hubert waved to the crowd as he spoke to the two of us
in a stage whisper.

"Get on my back, quick!"

We did as the dragon asked. Once we were firmly in
place, Hubert backed away from the throng. "Thank you!
Thank you!" he called. "You're a beautiful audience!"

Most of the crowd were calling for encores, save for
Dewey and Ferdie, who seemed to be saying things like
"That would hit the spot!" and "My compliments to the
chef!" I noticed Uncle Spike again as well, leading a
lavender dragon who I assumed was Aunt Louise. Both
Spike and Louise were watching me all too intently.

"Bye!" Hubert called to the throng. "Until we see you
again!" He turned to us. "Always leave them wanting
more."

The crowd called to us in a frenzy:

"Sure enough. The black horse was two inches taller
than the white horse!"

"Yeah, but we need the eggs!"

"Oh, nothing. Worms can't talk!"

"Wrapping paper!"

"Oh, sure. Just after I got it all tired out!"

"Oh, my God! I shot a nun!"

Hubert paused in his flight to survey the upturned faces
of the crowd below him.

"Gee," he called below, "do you think I should have
said Joe DiMaggio?"

Then he turned again, and we rose, with a great flapping
of wings.

We were on our way to heaven.

TWELVE

The concept of heaven is many different things to many different species. To a troll, it would be edible. To a giant, it might be a short distance overhead, right up that beanstalk over there. And to a unicorn, heaven consists of wherever that particular beast happens to be at that particular moment. And where is heaven for wizards? Well, that's a concept many of my fellows are still working on, but I assure you that that little tax-exempt retirement home overlooking the pleasure district of Vushta is at least on the proper road.

—From *The Teachings of Ebenezum*,
Special Weekly Update, Number 306

"Now, let's see," Hubert mused. "It's got to be around here someplace." The reptile exhaled. "At least it better be. There's not much strength left in these old wings."

We had flown up, and a little to the left, for quite some time. The home of the dragons had receded into the distance, now no more than a spec on the great curve of the globe beneath us. For the world below now looked like nothing so much as a giant sphere, and all the rivers and oceans and mountains therein looked like no more than insignificant lines and blotches and tiny spots scratched upon that great surface.

We must be nearing the home of the gods.

The air around us had changed of late, as Hubert flew even higher. When we had left the mountaintop of the dragon's home behind, we had left the clouds as well, and had flown through a vast expanse of open air. Now, however, we approached another cloudy region, although this vaporous shroud seemed far different from the fog and storm clouds below. Indeed, this new vista before us was incredibly white and fluffy, although very dense as well, as if something might be hidden on the other side.

"Look!" Hubert called excitedly. He pointed to a dark speck among the clouds overhead.

"Indeed," I replied. "What are we looking at?"

"Directions!" Hubert shouted.

And I saw, as we flew closer, that the speck was a sign, somehow attached to the bottom of a cloud. I squinted in an attempt to read the words.

"ALL DELIVERIES TO REAR DOOR."

Beneath those words was an arrow, pointing left. The dragon changed his course slightly to follow these new directions.

"Indeed!" I yelled forward toward Hubert's ear. "Is this the way we should be going? We're not exactly delivering anything!"

"But certainly we are!" Snarks objected. "We are delivering our fondest wishes to Plaugg, the slightly splendiferous!"

"Besides," the dragon reminded me, "it's not as if we were invited up here. Who knows how the keepers of the heavenly gates are going to react to our arrival? If we have any hopes of getting in here at all, I think the service entrance is by far our best bet."

"Indeed," I said, impressed by the remarkably thoughtful consideration my companions were giving to our present situation. I supposed that approaching heaven might bring that out in one. "I don't want to incur anybody's wrath, either," I added.

It seemed to me that was the sort of reaction you got from gods—wrath, floods, retribution, that sort of thing.

"I think we're getting close," Hubert called back again. "Thank goodness—these wings are weary!"

And, in fact, the nature of the clouds above us was changing, for while they were still as fleecy as before, they seemed to be graying as we passed beneath them, getting definitely dingy in spots, as though they had been smudged here and there. It was as if this area of cloud cover was used rather more than the rest, and not nearly as frequently washed.

"Another sign," Hubert rumbled.

Sure enough, there was a flat, brown area on the cloud immediately overhead, as if someone had set a door in the midst of the vapor. And on this door were large red letters: "R AR DOO"

"Rar doo?" Sparks inquired.

It puzzled me for a second as well.

"Indeed," I said after a moment's reflection. "If you added two letters, the sign would become 'REAR DOOR.' "

"You can tell why this fellow's our leader!" Hubert enthused. "If this is the rear door, then this is where we must go. Shall I knock?"

I told him I didn't see any reason why not. Hubert did as he was bade.

He waited a moment. There was no answer.

"There has to be somebody home!" Snarks insisted. "I mean, this is heaven, isn't it?"

"Indeed," I replied. "Hubert, why don't you knock a little louder?"

"Anything you say," Hubert agreed. "It's time for a real dragon knock!" He clenched his forepaw into a fist and drew it back as far as it would go.

"Yoo-hoo!" he called as he sent his fist crashing forward.

The door burst open.

"Oh, dear," Hubert remarked. "Do you think I broke it?"

"Should things even break in heaven?" Snarks asked. "Somehow, it would seem to be against the rules."

"Broken or not," I interjected, "I suggest we fly inside."

"True enough," Hubert answered as he fluttered his wings for one final effort. "We can worry about the niceties once we are on the other side."

We flew through the open trapdoor, into a very bright light.

The first thing I noticed was the sound of a choir, a thousand soprano voices singing at the top of their range. The next thing I saw, and it was very well lit up here, was a road of golden brick that wound its way through the clouds.

"Oof!"

Hubert landed, rather less gracefully than usual, at the beginning of the road, which, upon closer inspection, seemed to be made of regular bricks painted gold. I could tell because the paint had flaked off here and there, especially on the end of the road nearest the door. And in that small space between the road and the door was another sign, hand-lettered and slightly faded: "Please close door when you are finished."

"Hubert," I said, pointing to the sign. "Do you think we should?"

The dragon nodded. "It's only polite." He reached over and swung the door shut.

"Congratulations!" a voice boomed over the constant singing. *"You have passed the test!"*

When the three of us were done jumping and cowering, I noticed a small fellow, dressed in a rather colorless tunic, standing on the far side of the now closed door.

"Pardon," I asked, "but are you speaking to us?"

The small fellow smiled. "Don't see anybody else around here, do you?"

"Meaning no disrespect," I added hastily, "but no, we don't."

"Then I must be talking to you," the fellow concluded.

"Indeed," I replied. This fellow didn't seem to be very direct. I wondered how far I could question him without incurring his wrath, if indeed he was a god.

"Pardon me," I began again, "but would you mind telling us who you are?"

"Not at all!" the fellow answered. "As you see, this is the delivery entrance. And I am, of course, Devino, the god of delivery entrances. That's the way things work up here."

"And we have passed the test?" I ventured.

"I just said that, didn't I?" the god of delivery entrances replied with a grin. "You can't let just anybody into heaven. However, seeing you close the door behind you, I know you're the right sort."

"Seems like an awfully simple test," Snarks muttered.

Devino sighed and nodded. "Actually, when you're the god of delivery entrances, there aren't too many tests you can perform. But you're here now, and you may enter heaven."

I thanked the deity, and asked him if he might be able to direct us to the home of Plaugg.

"The overwhelmingly adequate," Snarks added reverentially.

"You're in luck," the delivery deity said. He pointed down the road. "Plaugg lives just past that cloud. First mansion on the right."

We thanked the deity and began our walk down the heavenly road. Hubert remarked on how happy he was to be able to move his feet for a change.

The clouds bordered the bricks on either side, looking like nothing so much as snow-covered hills, as if this landscape was as substantial as the world we had come from down below. And who knew, perhaps it was, for we were in a special place with special rules. I had been across large parts of the earth below, and had even ventured beneath the ground to the fearsome realms of the Netherhells. But never had I found myself in a place so wondrously strange as this, the home of all the gods.

Still, I could do no less than venture here, for the sake of Ebenezum. It was all so different, and so unreal. But we were mere steps from our goal! And with Plaugg's assistance, perhaps I would be able to save my master at last!

"Watch where you're walking!" a voice bellowed.

Hubert, Snarks and I stopped abruptly. Sound certainly had a way of carrying up here.

Ahead of us stood another fellow, a little larger than the god of delivery entrances, and a little pudgier. He also wore a tunic, although his garment seemed to have gold threads worked into the colorless fabric, which made the cloth somehow simultaneously drab and glistening. This new deity pointed to a sign by his side.

Caution!
DEITIES AT WORK
Road legally closed.

"And we mean it!" the fellow added. "Oh, sorry. I didn't intend to bellow in your ears. It's simply all this stress I've been under lately."

"Indeed?" I asked, seeking to learn the nature of this god.

"I should say so," the deity replied. "They don't realize what a full-time job this is, especially with people wanting to use these roads all the time!"

"Then you work on the roads?"

"What else have I got time to do?" the deity laughed bitterly. "Oh, sorry. I should probably introduce myself. I am Devano, the god of brick roads painted with gold flake. With a job like that, I'm obviously stuck in the lower reaches of heaven!"

"Indeed," I commented, "and you're working on this particular road?"

"You read the sign?" Devano replied moodily. "This gold flake takes constant upkeep! It's not like those real gold roads uptown."

"Uptown?" Snarks asked.

"Yeah, you know, the posh neighborhoods—Pantheon Heights, Olympus Manor, places like that. But do you think they could be bothered to put in those gold roads down here?"

"I'm sure it is quite a problem," I agreed. "However, we must travel farther up this road for a very important meeting with a deity. Is there any possibility we might be able to get through?"

Devano frowned. "The paint job's pretty new. You two small fellows could probably get through without causing too much damage, but if I'm not mistaken, one of you is a dragon."

"That's quite correct," Hubert rumbled.

"Of course I'm correct," Devano said brusquely. "I'm a deity."

"Indeed," I interjected again. "We intend no disrespect—"

"I should hope not!" Devano insisted. "We don't want any wraths incurred around here, do we?"

"What kind of wrath could a gold-flake painter have?" Snarks asked before I could stop him.

"Would you like to be bronzed?" Devano muttered darkly. "Or perhaps gilding would suit you better? It can be arranged."

"I fear we do not desire either bronzing or gilding," I replied. "What we need is to travel up this road until we find Plaugg."

"The tolerably resplendent," Snarks added.

"Sorry," Devano asserted. "The reptile makes one step on that road, and it's wrathtime!"

"Maybe I could walk around," Hubert suggested, nodding toward the surrounding cloud hills.

The deity shook his head. "They'd never take his weight. It's a problem living someplace as insubstantial as this. And it's a long way down."

"And my wings are in no shape for that kind of exercise," Hubert moaned.

"Unfortunately, we must go on ahead," I stated. "We must see Plaugg—"

"The reasonably radiant," Snarks interjected.

"—for the sake of my master!" I concluded.

"Well, what will become of me?" Hubert asked, a hint of trepidation in his voice.

"You'll have to stay behind," Snarks said bluntly, "with the gold-flake god here."

"It won't be so bad," Devano assured him. "I haven't

had anyone to discuss brick painting technique with in ever so long.''

"Brick painting technique?" Hubert asked. "I'm sure it would be fascinating, but on second thought, my wings have gotten all sorts of rest in the last few minutes. Up, up, and—uh—away!"

And with that, Hubert raised himself a half dozen paces above the road.

"Don't land before the intersection up ahead!" Devano called. "Or it's wrath city!"

"Yes, sir, Your Deityship, sir," Hubert groaned. He flew on ahead, his face wrinkled in a very unpleasant expression.

"May we go as well?" I asked the god.

"Certainly," Devano answered. "As long as you keep over to the left. That's the side I painted first."

I thanked the god of painting gold flake on brick roads, and we resumed our journey in silence, the only sounds those distant, ethereal, never-ending voices. We caught up with Hubert a few moments later. The dragon was breathing heavily, collapsed on the spot where the golden road branched in three directions.

"I don't use—those wing muscles—enough anymore!" Hubert gasped. "As of now—for the foreseeable future—flying is right out!"

"Indeed," I reassured the reptile, even though I wondered: Without Hubert's flying help, how would we get out of here once we were done with Plaugg?

I asked the other question that was on my mind instead. "Which way is it to Plaugg's?"

"The spectacularly so-so," Snarks added.

"Pardon?" another voice boomed all around.

After the three of us had managed to quiet our jumping hearts, we looked for the owner of the overwhelming voice. No matter how many times it happened, this call-out-of-nowhere business had never ceased to be disconcerting. A tunicked figure waved from the middle road.

"Heard you had a little trouble!" the newcomer called. This time, we only cowered for a moment. "Oh, sorry. Booming voices come with the territory. It's the only way

we can hear each other over the stupid music you always hear playing." The high, soprano voices hummed happily in the background. "And if you think it's bad around here, you should go over to the shopping mall."

"Pardon?" I asked. I had heard of these "shopping malls." Wasn't that something they had in the Netherhells?

"But that's beside the point," the newcomer continued. "I have come here to help you find your way."

"Indeed?" I inquired.

"Exactly. I am Devoono, god of showing wanderers the way through the byways of the lower reaches of heaven."

"That's all?" Snarks asked.

Devoono nodded. "It is a rather specialized calling, I grant you, but it has its rewards."

"Like what?" Snarks demanded.

"Well, for one thing, I don't have to paint bricks," Devoono answered. "But I heard that you travelers have lost your way?"

"Indeed," I replied, glad that this fellow was in a much better mood than the last deity we had come across. "We need to locate Plaugg."

"The incredibly inconsequential," Snarks chimed in.

"Easy enough." Devoono pointed down the far right road. "Walk down there. It's the first mansion, well, the first dwelling, you'll come to."

"That close?" I mused. "How can we possibly thank you?"

But the deity just nodded pleasantly. "Think nothing of it. It's better than sitting around a delivery entrance all day!"

Then he disappeared without a sound.

"It's a little disconcerting around here," Hubert remarked.

"Are you kidding?" Snarks sneered. "It's a *lot* disconcerting around here. Give me the molten slime pits of the Netherhells any day. At least there you know when something's going to come out and grab you!"

"Indeed," I interjected. "I believe it is time we went and grabbed Plaugg."

"The incredibly indifferent," Snarks added.

"If you will follow me?" I suggested, turning down the right-hand golden road.

The dwelling came in sight almost immediately, and I could see why the deity we had spoken with most recently had hesitated calling it a mansion. For, while it was reasonably large, it was not without its problems. To put it charitably, it needed a little work. The massive pillars to either side of the door were slightly askew, there were cracks here and there in the numerous statues, and there seemed to be piles of orange, spongy stuff littering the front walk.

It was a wondrous place, gone ever so slightly to seed. I had never seen a building at once so ordinary and so magnificent. Even if Devoono hadn't shown us the way, there would have been no mistaking it.

It had to be the mansion of Plaugg.

THIRTEEN

Etiquette is as important to wizards as it is to anyone else. Say, for example, that one of your numerous visiting in-laws criticizes the upkeep of the home. You, of course, should smile graciously at this remark, and pleasantly reply that you will be more than glad to turn them into a broom.

—From *Ask Ebenezum:*
A Handy Compendium of Wizards' Do's and Don'ts,
fourth edition,
by Ebenezum,
greatest wizard in the Western Kingdoms

We walked up to the front door, which appeared to be a bit loose on its hinges.

"Shall I?" Hubert asked, his massive forepaw ready to knock.

"Actually," I remarked, "I believe the honor of announcing our presence should go to Snarks. After all, he's the member of our company who worships Plaugg."

"The ineptly unequaled," Snarks whispered, awed by his surroundings. "Who thought I would ever be here, at the tumbledown mansion of *Him*?"

"So are you going to knock?" Hubert prompted.

The demon blinked and stared at the large reptile. "That's the problem with dragons. No sense of the true proprieties. I shall knock when I am spiritually prepared."

Snarks took a deep breath and knocked.

A woman's voice answered.

"We don't want any!"

Snarks took a step away. "Are you sure this is the right place?"

"Indeed," I replied. "At least that last deity said so."

"That must mean that Plaugg does not live in solitude!" Snarks shivered with the thought. "The theological implications alone are staggering."

"We're still not inside," Hubert reminded the demon. "We still have to see this guy."

"This guy?" Snarks exploded. "You refer to *Him* as 'this guy'? I'll have you know that Plaugg, bless His magnificently mediocre name, is the *Ultimate* Guy!"

"Indeed," I said soothingly. "Perhaps you should knock again."

Snarks smoothed his robes, calming himself with an effort.

"You are right, of course," the demon said at last. "I am ever so slightly overwrought, being so close—"

He stopped talking and knocked.

"We gave at the office!" the voice shouted.

"No, madam!" I called back. "You misunderstand. We are here seeking the wisdom of Plaugg!"

"Seeking his *what*?" the woman yelled. "Now I *know* you're at the wrong house." I heard the sound of feet scuffling across flagstone. "Oh, very well. I suppose I have to humor the old deity. Wait a moment and I'll lift the latch."

The door made a creaking sound and swung wide. There was no one on the other side.

"Come on in if you're coming!" the woman's voice called. "You can't keep deities waiting all day!"

Snarks and I stepped gingerly inside, crossing a cracked marble foyer into a very large room in severe need of cleaning.

"Plaugg!" the voice shouted. "Believe it or not, there's somebody here to see you."

"What?" a somewhat confused-sounding male voice called back. "Oh, very well. I'll be there in a minute."

Snarks looked wonderingly about the rather dingy but immense room we found ourselves in. "You know who that was," he whispered. "Plaugg!"

"The miraculously tardy," the disembodied woman's voice added. "He's bad enough as it is. You should be careful not to encourage him."

"Here I come! Here I come!" A fellow who was even shorter and more nondescript than the last couple deities we had met brushed aside a large cobweb and stepped into the room from one of the many surrounding alcoves. "Give me a minute now to adjust my robes." He fumbled with his tunic, which seemed rather grayer than those of others we had seen. He tugged his clothes three inches along one shoulder, frowned, then tugged them back the other way.

"There," he said at last, although I could see no difference. "That will have to do. Now, what seems to be the problem?"

Snarks fell to his knees. Even I remembered this remarkably nondescript deity from that day, so long ago, when he saved us from the Netherhells. It was Plaugg.

"Oh, Your Nondescriptness," Snarks groveled. "This is such an honor, Your Unremarkableness. How do I begin—"

"Pardon me," Plaugg interrupted, "but aren't you a demon?"

"Why, yes, Your Insipidness," Snarks stammered, "here to—um—"

"I thought as much, Plaugg replied proudly. "I'm a deity, you know. Things like this rarely escape my notice."

"Really?" the woman's voice remarked. "Then why don't you notice things around the house?"

"Now, dearest," Plaugg said with a frown. "I'm sure these nice pilgrims don't want to hear about—"

"Well, I don't want to hear about it, either!" the other

voice exclaimed. "But how else am I going to get you to listen—"

"Dearest," Plaugg replied firmly. "Now is not the time or place. And why don't you manifest yourself for these nice people? It's not very polite, hanging around the room like that and making declarations from the ether."

"Oh, I suppose you're right," the woman agreed. "For once."

A light gray cloud coalesced at the center of the room. Plaugg turned back to Snarks.

"We don't get many demons up here."

"We don't get much of anybody up here!" declared the woman's voice, now attached to a form which, besides being female, was of much the same stature and shape as Plaugg. "I mean, who would want to come to a place like this?"

"Now, Devuna," Plaugg cautioned.

But, once started, the goddess was not so easily stopped. "Why don't you look at this dump? Everything in this place needs to be cleaned up and repaired. And the outside? Hah! You can barely call our home a mansion anymore, it needs so much work."

"You're becoming overwrought, dear—" Plaugg began.

"Overwrought?" Devuna laughed caustically. "Tell me this! When's the last time you swept the manna off the sidewalk?"

"Oh, my, is it piling up again?" Plaugg said distractedly. "That's one of the problems with living in a place where foodstuffs fall from the void." The god glanced at Snarks and myself. "You folks wouldn't want any, would you? It's quite tasty. Nutritious, too."

"Indeed," I replied, for it seemed time for someone to take action so that this conversation did not wander aimlessly forever. "Perhaps we will try a bit later, but now we must ask for your assistance."

"Yes, Your Prosaicness," Snarks piped up. " 'Tis the very thing that I, as Your worshipper, have been trying to put into words, if only I could find . . ." The demon's voice trailed off.

"See?" Plaugg pointed out to his spouse. "They need my assistance!"

The goddess snorted. "Good luck with them getting it!"

Plaugg turned apologetically back to Snarks and myself. "You'll have to excuse my wife, Devuna. I'm afraid, when a couple lives together throughout eternity, these little problems can creep up."

"Little?" Devuna exploded. "You call that constant drip, drip, drip in the sink a *little* problem?"

"Well, perhaps not, but you know the trouble I have there," Plaugg defended himself. "I have to find the time to study the problem, so that I might discover exactly the right motion for deific repair of that sort. After all, if I make the gesture in the proper direction, the leak is gone. However, should I inadvertently reverse the move, the waters of the heavens descend upon us." He spread his hands in a gesture of helplessness. "You can see my problem, can't you?"

Devuna grunted in dismissal. I, however, could certainly sympathize with the deity, having been in many similar situations myself.

Plaugg sighed, nodding sadly. "Sometimes, being a deity is more of a problem than it's worth."

"We appreciate Your concerns, Your So-soness," Snarks spoke up, "but, if we might, we could use a moment of Your reasonably valuable time."

Plaugg smiled at the demon. "Anything for my worshippers. By the way, that's a dragon looking through the doorway, isn't it?"

"Pleased to meet you!" Hubert called.

"We don't get many dragons up here," Plaugg admitted.

"We're never going to have anybody up here ever again," his wife insisted, "if you don't do some work around the place." She glared at her god-husband. "And that *anybody* includes good-for-nothing deities!"

"Indeed," I spoke to the goddess, seeking to distract her so that Snarks might properly petition Plaugg. "You are Devuna?"

"And proud of it!" Devuna sniffed. "I am the goddess of put-upon wives whose names begin with *P*, *Q* and *R*."

"Indeed?" I replied.

"Exactly," she answered. "The job had so many worshippers, we had to divide up the duties."

"I had no idea," I continued, "that the deity business was so specialized."

"It's the modern way." She shot another incriminating look at her husband. "Everyone's got a specialty, except Plaugg!"

"Someone's got to be a general practitioner!" Plaugg shot back. "It's a tradition up here in the Elysian fields."

"Tradition—smadition!" His wife carped. She glanced back at me. "The simple truth is that Plaugg is incapable of making decisions."

"I can too make decisions!" Plaugg exclaimed. "At least, I think I can."

"Oh, Your Nothing-Specialness!" Snarks interjected. "Please hear us out, for, with every passing moment, our situation is getting worse!"

"Quite right," Plaugg agreed. "Devuna and I have all eternity to argue, a fact I sometimes attempt to forget. Tell me now, petitioners: What is your problem?"

Together, Snarks and I briefly outlined what had happened so far: how Death had decided that I was the Eternal Apprentice; how Death coveted my soul which—because I was the Eternal Apprentice—until now had been unobtainable; how I had thus far managed to avoid the fiend in that selfsame quest for my soul; how my master had been spirited to the land of Death by that treacherous specter, so that I would be expected to exchange my own life for that of the wizard; and how I had to find a way to rescue Ebenezum without sacrificing myself.

"Oh, of course!" Plaugg stated. "I knew that. Being a deity, I am somewhat omnipotent, you know."

"Then, might You help us, Your Adequateness?" Snarks implored.

Plaugg considered for a second. "Anything for a worshipper—"

He paused again as Snarks and I exchanged grins.

"—within limits," he concluded.

"What did I tell you?" Devuna interposed. "Nothing but talk, talk, talk."

"Now, now, dearest," Plaugg chided. "There's actually quite a lot I can do. It will simply take me a little time to do it." He glanced distractedly at Snarks and me. "Somehow, we need to get you into the Kingdom of Death. I am, unfortunately, not properly informed on methods to transport worshippers into totally different spheres of existence." He smiled apologetically. "I'm afraid I have enough trouble getting around myself."

"He never leaves the house," Devuna agreed. "Can't even get him to run a simple errand."

"Now, now," Plaugg contradicted. "That's not precisely true. It's simply that I have to watch my movements. Should I walk one way, I can go down to the corner and pick up some groceries. However, should my movements inadvertently change mid-errand, I could alter the very fabric of the cosmos." He shrugged exhaustedly. "No one truly appreciates the problems of a deity."

"Excuses, always excuses," Devuna muttered.

"Least of all my wife," Plaugg concluded. "Now, how soon must you rescue this wizard?" He stared into space for an instant, his lips moving silently, then returned his gaze to Snarks and myself. "Would two weeks from Wednesday be sufficient?"

"B-but, Your Unexceptionalness!" Snarks stammered. "That cannot—" His voice died, the demon unable to contradict his deity.

"Indeed," I added helpfully. "It may already be too late—"

Plaugg's laughter held a touch of embarrassment. "Oh, that's right, you did say it was urgent. It's just that, when you're a deity, why, you tend to have simply *everything* on your mind! An immediate solution, hmm?"

"Unfortunately true, Your Passableness!" Snarks replied. "We must reach the Kingdom of Death with all speed."

Plaugg sighed. "Speed, huh? I don't know if I can help you there."

"You can say that again!" Devuna interjected.

"Of course," Plaugg added uncertainly, "you could take a tour bus—"

"Indeed," I said. "A tour bus?" I was unfamiliar with the heavenly term.

"What an idea!" Devuna exclaimed, new admiration in her voice. "A tour bus would get them down there in no time at all. Every once in a while, you remind me why I married you."

"Think nothing of it," Plaugg remarked self-deprecatingly.

"I usually don't," Devuna answered with a smile.

"Dearest," Plaugg prompted, "you wouldn't happen to have a schedule?"

The goddess frowned. "You're right. I do have one around here someplace." She furrowed her brow, and a piece of parchment materialized in her hand. She studied the newfound paper for an instant. "We're in luck. The Kingdom of Death Express leaves in seventeen minutes!"

"Indeed," I said again, totally confused. "A tour bus?"

"Don't worry," Plaugg assured me. "I'll take care of everything. Which gate does it leave from, dearest?"

"Oh, that's right," Devuna nodded in sudden understanding. "Pearly is closed down for construction." She looked down to the bottom of her parchment. "All tours are temporarily leaving from Celestial."

"Celestial it is." Plaugg smiled. "I'll have you there in a jiffy." He paused to wave at the dragon in the doorway. "All three of you. And if you need anything else, all you have to do is ask. That's what I'm here for. I can hear most anything, which can be a bit of a problem sometimes, let me tell you. However, since I know you'll be calling, I'll be listening. Now, let's see—" He bit his lower lip in concentration.

"Does this mean you're going to be making house calls again?" his wife demanded.

"In a minute, dearest." Plaugg frowned.

"He can make house calls," Devuna muttered distractedly, "but can he sweep the steps? Sometimes—"

"I've got it!" Plaugg cried triumphantly. "Have a nice tour! Don't forget to write!"

The deity's voice faded as Snarks and I were surrounded by smoke. My companions and I were to be sent to the "tour bus," whatever that was.

But one thing was certain. We were going at last to rescue my master! My joy would have been complete, save for one thought:

Once we got to the Kingdom of Death, what would we do next?

FOURTEEN

*I am reminded of an amusing incident that oc-
curred early in my career. A certain spell had been
intended to increase a king's knowledge, but through
a small error on my part, had instead doubled the
size of everyone's nose within the kingdom. I attempted to apologize to the angry throng when the
king, whose nose had been none too small to begin
with, rushed upon the scene with the royal executioner in tow, and demanded a satisfactory conclusion
of our business, or else.*

*The angry mob, however, who couldn't have cared
less about royalty getting their money's worth, re-
volted, storming the castle and grabbing me away
from the executioner's blade. After a couple more
minor errors, I managed to set things right with the
majority of the population, especially with regards to
nose size, although I did neglect to extend the anti-
dote spell to the monarch.*

*And so I left that particular land, but—and I think
this proves I am a fair wizard—not before I had
written an anonymous note, advising the king that, if
he were to properly weight his crown in the back, it
would aid in balancing his head so that his chin was
not constantly resting on his chest.*

Now, what is the point of this little tale? Consider

*this: How else might I get rescued by an angry mob
an instant before being murdered by a vengeful king?
I think the moral is obvious. It always pays to advertise.*

—From *Wake Up and Conjure!:*
The Collected Speeches of Ebenezum,
Greatest Wizard in the Western Kingdoms,
Volume CCCXII,
The Year of the Demon,
the first three weeks of summer

"Watch your step!"

The smoke had cleared abruptly. I was standing at the
foot of a subtly vibrating stairway.

"Hurry it up, would you, please?" said a fellow standing by my side. He wore a gray robe and matching cap.
"I've got a schedule to keep. And I need that ticket."

Ticket? Oh, I realized, the fellow must be referring to
the square of parchment I held in my hand. I passed it to
him.

"Good enough," the gray fellow said as he pointed up
the stairs. "Sit wherever you like on the bus."

I carefully ascended the barely jiggling stairway as the
fellow spoke to Snarks.

"Ticket? Say, you're a demon, aren't you?"

Snarks complimented the fellow's perceptiveness.

"We don't get many demons on this tour. Actually, we
don't get much of anybody on this tour. It's a popular
misconception that a tour of the Kingdom of the Dead
might be downright depressing! Well, let me tell you right
now, with me behind the wheel, it's anything but! Hop on
the bus, now!"

I heard Snark's feet behind me as I reached the top of
the stairs.

"Wait a second, mac," declared the fellow who was
apparently our guide. "This may be a heavenly bus, but
there's no way we can fit a dragon in here!"

I looked back down the stairs past Snarks. Hubert tipped
his top hat and showed the fellow his ticket.

"Okay, okay," the guide said with a frown. He pointed overhead. "I guess you can ride on top."

"The proper place for a dragon," Hubert rumbled as he clambered on top of whatever this thing was that I now stood inside.

"That's it, then?" the guide called, looking hopefully about the cloud fields that surrounded this "bus." "This is your last chance!" he added.

He was answered by silence.

"Everybody in their seats, then!" he called up to us. "It's time for the tour!"

Snarks joined me at the top of the stairs. I turned to look down a long aisle, bordered on either side by padded benches. The rest of this "bus" was empty—we had been the first to climb within it. I sat on the second bench from the front, next to a large, covered window. Snarks sat on my other side.

"A tour bus?" the demon whispered in wonder. "Surely, this is one of the mystic engines of the gods."

The guide jumped up the steps two at a time and sat at a small bench at the very front of the enclosed interior. He did something with his hands. We were surrounded by a rumbling, like distant thunder.

"Welcome!" the guide's voice boomed even though he faced away from us. "On a heavenly tour you will never forget!"

There was a tapping at my window. I turned, and saw Hubert's upside-down face grinning at me.

"I hope everyone is quite comfortable in their seats," the guide continued, "because here we go!"

There was a whooshing sound, like we were surrounded by a great wind, and we were no longer in heaven. We were surrounded by blue sky, far above the world.

"I'm Devorno, your divine driver," our guide continued. "And I'll be showing you some of the sights on our trip beyond the realm of the living! That's right! I guess you could say there's any number of things I'll be dying to tell you! Ha, ha, ha!"

Snarks blanched where he sat by my side. "Does this guy know Hubert?" he whispered.

I knew instantly what the demon meant. There was a certain awfulness about the driver's humor that was immediately recognizable.

"But this bus does more than fly through the air," Devorno continued. "Now, when I pull this cord here, this magic carriage will send us sailing through a dozen different realms of existence, straight to our goal, the Kingdom of Death. Look carefully, now. On a trip like this, you never know what you might see!"

The driver pulled the cord.

The light changed again, going from deep red to brilliant yellow to blinding white, as if we were flying into the heart of the sun. Then, as quickly as the light flared, it was gone, replaced by a soft golden glow. And in that glow stood at least a hundred women. What's more, all of them were staring at me. Wasn't that Alea in the corner? The women all opened their mouths to speak at the same time, and said a single word in unison. Could that be Norei that we just passed? I realized with a start what that single word had been. All the women had spoken my name.

"There they are," the driver interjected, "all the women that you might ever love. A part of each of them waits for you in this realm of possibilities, as you wait for them elsewhere. Just think, your life could be spent with any one of these beauties. Now, that's what I call living!"

So it was an image of Norei I saw! And Alea as well. But all those women? After I had already discovered my own true love? Surely it was some mistake. I turned to ask Snarks his opinion, but found him staring out the window, openmouthed.

"I've never seen so many female demons in one place!" he whispered.

"Female demons?" I replied. "Indeed." Apparently, on this edge of heaven, each of us saw only that which pertained to him specifically. I wondered if the same held true for the dragon who rode on top. But then I heard Hubert's tail thumping on the roof overhead.

"But we have to say goodbye to our lovely ladies," the driver's voice broke into my thoughts, "for we are passing into another place altogether."

The lighting changed from golden to palest blue. But that was not all that differed, for the landscape was now crowded with people: thousands upon thousands, men, women and children of all sizes, types and ages; so many that the very ground upon which they stood seemed to sag beneath their numbers. And among them, again, were those that I recognized, including a giant and a dragon.

"This place is almost empty," Snarks complained as he stared out the window beside me.

"Yes, gentlemen," the driver continued, "in this place are arrayed your life's companions. All those with whom you might form a bond, as indeed, in other realms, you wait as a companion for others."

But there were thousands of them out there!

"Six?" Snarks whispered. "That's all I'm ever going to get is—six companions? Plus, I know half of them already. You're out there; I'd recognize that terrible posture anywhere. And that fellow wearing the breastplate that should house two or three—well, that was to be Hendrek. But wait—there's someone else moving out there, someone so small I almost missed him. So small?" A look of horror overtook the demon's countenance. "It could not be! He couldn't be a companion of mine! Not—the Brownie!"

"I'm bringing the laces now—" Tap mumbled from where he rested, deep within my pocket. The words were followed by a soft snoring.

"Indeed," I replied, for what now happened here gave me much to think about. I saw thousands from the window, while Snarks perhaps saw seven. What could account for this discrepancy? Perhaps I was truly the Eternal apprentice, after all. Why else would I have so many and the demon so few?

"The Brownie?" Snarks whispered again. "Is there any way to send companions back?"

Well, it was either that I was the Eternal apprentice, I further conjectured, or Snarks's nature was such that he annoyed almost everyone he met, thus keeping his companions to the barest minimum. Perhaps this quandary was unsolvable.

Hubert was making some consistent noise on the roof above us. After a moment's conjecture, I decided it was a soft shoe.

"But we leave this realm behind as well," the guide's voice boomed, "as we move into a more dangerous corner of the cosmos."

The light changed again, this time shifting to an angry red glow. I saw others, arrayed across the celestial countryside we passed, although this time they did not look so friendly. In fact, they looked rather more like monsters and demons of the most unsavory kind.

"We pass now," the guide continued, "and very quickly, may I add, through the region of danger and fear. All your problems wait out there for you, gentlemen, and would be only too happy to get a chance at you now, rather than waiting until their proper time. Lucky for us, though, this bus is beyond their reach. It's a little feature we have called climate control."

I could not take my eyes off the fiends that we passed. I realized I had faced some of them before, both with my sword, Cuthbert, and with my stout oak staff. That must mean that I might have to face the many others sometime in the future.

Or perhaps I would not have to face any more of them, save one, for in the very center of the fiends stood Death, laughing.

"But that's enough of that," our guide interjected. "And now, as the heavenly shores recede farther into the distance, we pass through a few realms that are not so personal. Sit back and relax, as you see things not quite of the world below or this world above."

The guide's voice was replaced by that high choir music we had heard all over heaven.

The colors outside the bus changed again, then yet again, as if the vehicle was speeding us through many places on our way to our destination. Sights flashed by our window at lightning speed, at first portraying scenes of knights and heroes, as you might see on tapestries, then changing to more fantastic themes, as if we had once again returned to the fairy tales of the Eastern Kingdoms. And then the sights grew stranger still. A group of men wearing helmets and immense amounts of padding fought in the mud over a small brown ovoid. A second group of men holding sticks chased a small round stone around the ice. What was the meaning of these strange activities? A third group of very tall men wearing only their underwear bounced this large ball, occasionally crashing into each other as one of them tossed the ball into the air. Then the scene shifted again, and two very large men faced each other in a roped-off square, both leaping and grabbing, each man trying to get an advantage over the other.

Ah, but I knew what happened now! This was wrestling, the most popular sport in all of the Western Kingdoms! Then were those other, much stranger activities sports as well? But how could any other sport have the honesty and true excitement of the art of grappling? I was destined never to know, for the lighting shifted again.

This seemed to be a quieter realm, mostly made up of strangely garbed people engaged in earnest conversation, although, for some odd reason, the colors had become more intense than in any realm we had seen before. But there were flashes of other things as well: large containers of what appeared to be food and drink, and conveyances smaller than the bus we now rode in, but somehow related— these vehicles were almost always painted red, and seemed to come with a fair damsel seated within as these little buses moved all too fast down twisting roads.

The faces grew larger as I watched people cough and sneeze. My interest increased, for I hoped I might catch a glimpse of my master, but I saw naught but pictures of strange bottles and boxes, covered by pictures and lettering that were stranger still.

A giant head appeared from nowhere, accompanied by a voice so loud that it penetrated the window that separated us:

"I had a headache *this* big—"

"Whoops!" the guide called back to us. "We've gotten a little off course here. But don't worry, folks, I just have to make a slight correction, and we'll be in the Kingdom of Death in no time!"

The guide pulled another pair of cords. The bus shook. I heard a faint squealing sound from somewhere. All of the intense colors vanished, to be replaced by a world of gray.

I didn't need the guide to tell us where we were now. We had arrived in the Kingdom of Death.

FIFTEEN

*I have always sworn by the wisdom of traveling
with companions. In dangerous situations, the more
companions you have, the more secure you will feel.
Thus, should you be faced with a sudden attack by
some fearsome beast of the forest, you will be better
able to defend yourself if you have a companion or
two by your side, rather than having to face the
danger alone. Similarly, should you be the victim of a
surprise attack by the Netherhells, a dozen weapon-
wielding companions are more than welcome by your
side.*

*And what about companions for that moment when
you enter the Kingdom of Death? Well, let me put it
to you this way: have you ever wanted the entire city
of Vushta to be your friend?*

—From *Some Thoughts on Apprenticeship*,
    by Wuntvor, assistant to Ebenezum,
    greatest wizard in the Western Kingdoms
        (a work in progress)

"Doesn't look too lively around here, does it?" the guide's
cheer attempted, but failed, to penetrate the surrounding
gloom. "And little wonder, 'cause this is a dead town if

137

I've ever seen one! Ha, ha! Just kidding, folks. Yes, we've reached our destination, land of the big D! But the tour has only begun! In the next few minutes, we'll hit all the points of interest in this realm, and maybe, if we're lucky, get a glimpse of the head specter itself!''

So we would see Death? I supposed there was no avoiding a confrontation, now that we had entered his realm. Still, I wished there was some way I might contact my master before I grappled with the bony fiend.

I looked out the window, but there was no sign of Death yet. In fact, there was not much sign of anything at all. The landscape about us was colorless, and almost featureless, as if the whole of the space around was coated with a thin fog above a layer of gray snow. It was hard to make out anything in the dim light, but I thought I saw figures moving slowly through the distance, at that point where objects went from indistinct to invisible.

"We are traveling now through the Region of Unrelieved Grayness!" our guide explained. "At least that's what they call it hereabouts. With a name like that, it's no wonder property values around here are so low!"

"It's too bad we need this guy to take us to your master," Snarks whispered in my ear. "Otherwise, we could strangle him."

I softly replied that Snarks should contain himself. Any moment now, it would be time to leave this bus and guide behind. That's when the real danger would begin.

"But the Region of Unrelieved Grayness does not go on forever!" the guide announced happily. "No, we will pass beyond it in a moment to other parts of Death's kingdom. For the land of the dead is as varied as the souls that reside here, as varied as all the worlds the dead have come from, if not more so."

It became brighter outside as the guide spoke. The air was slowly clearing, and I could see hints of color through the haze, a faint blue here, a bit of pink there, a swatch of green close by the ground. Then, as if someone—or something—had snapped his fingers, the air cleared completely, and the view outside was as bright as noon on a summer's day, except, oddly enough, that I could see no sign of the sun. We had entered a place full of green grass and blue sky, and were approaching a pavilion of tents, each a different color, and each one somehow, impossibly, brighter than the one before.

"You will see, over on your left, one of Death's gaming areas," our guide continued. "We'll tour another of these later on, for they litter this realm. As some of you may know, Death is very fond of games."

I could not suppress a shudder. I was all too aware of Death's fondness for games. Up to this point, I had spent all my energy finding a way to reach my master. Now I would have to find a way to confront Death. What game would I have to play to rescue Ebenezum?

"There are places here that are not so different from the world you know, gentlemen," the guide's booming voice remarked. "In fact, we are now passing that part of Death's domain that most resembles the Western Kingdoms. As you can see, we are surrounded by unrelieved greenery. It's almost as dull as the real thing, isn't it, folks?"

Western Kingdoms? Dull? Maybe I should reconsider Snarks's offer to strangle this fellow.

"Why are these places here?" the guide continued rhetorically. "What is the reason for gray areas next door to regions of endless light? Who can truly fathom the world of the dead?" The bus divinity paused dramatically. "We may never know the answers to these questions. But perhaps we'll get some inklings about those secrets at our first stop, just ahead. And, as an extra bonus, you can get any of a number of mouth-watering refreshments as well!"

The bus turned sharply and stopped. We had pulled up next to a small wooden structure with a festively painted sign hung across the roof:

LAND OF THE DEAD
SOUVENIR SHOP
and Snack Bar
(Tourist Tips, Too!)
"All the Dead Stop Here"

Other, smaller signs covered the window below:

PETRIFIED WOOD INSIDE!

We can supply all your ash and dust needs!
420 varieties!

Inert Objects of Every Kind!
If it doesn't move, we've got it!

"Everybody out!" the guide announced. "And don't dawdle. The tour resumes in fifteen minutes." And with that, Devorno climbed down the steps and out of the bus.

"Shall we?" I asked the demon.

"I'll do anything to get away from here," Snarks replied.

I led the way out of the strange vehicle.

"It's quite something, isn't it?" Hubert rumbled from the top of the bus.

"Indeed," I said. "Then your journey was satisfactory?" I had to admit to myself that, in the heat of the tour, I had all but forgotten about Hubert crouching overhead. If I had not been so concerned for my master, I might have worried more for the dragon's safety.

"More than satisfactory!" the dragon enthused. "Once I got used to the sudden changes in scenery, it became inspirational!"

"Inspirational?" Snarks replied with a bit of trepidation. The demon climbed down to my side.

"Yes!" the dragon replied rapturously. "Just think of the song-and-dance routines that can come out of an experience like this. Something like—" Hubert cleared his throat and sang:

"You haven't lived until you've seen
The Kingdom of the Dead.
It's the sort of place to excite your spleen!
You heard what I said!
So go to the place that's really keen
Once your skin is shed
Don't waste time! Come on! Careen
To that Kingdom of the Dead!"

His jaw snapped shut as he looked to us for approval.

"Indeed," I remarked.

"Or something like that," he added. "After all, it's only a first draft."

"Indeed," I said again, digging my heels into the ground, which seemed as real as the earth beneath one's feet in the Western Kingdoms. "Should we go inside?"

"I think we have to," Snarks answered dryly. "At least, we do if we want to get our money's worth."

"If it's all right with you fellows," Hubert said, "I think I'll simply stay out here and *experience*!"

I nodded, and told Snarks to follow me, for I realized that there was another reason to go inside as well. Now that we had reached the Kingdom of Death, we had to find my master. What better place to start than an information center like this?

As I opened the door to the strange structure, I felt the Brownie stir in my pocket and mutter something about shining the buckles in a minute. Perhaps, I considered, now was the time to wake the sleeping Tap.

The door made a noise as I opened it: a sound halfway between a squeaking hinge and Death's dark laughter. It took me a second to realize that the specter wasn't waiting for me on the other side.

"That got your attention, didn't it?" Devorno shouted from across the room. "I tell you, Death is a marketing genius!"

Snarks frowned as he looked around the room, which seemed filled with piles of stones and dust. Signs stuck from the pile tops:

Dirt Cheap!
Everything Must Go!
Rock-bottom Prices!

"This is marketing genius?" the demon asked.

"Well," Devorno said, "perhaps this place is not the best example. But it is only one small piece of Death's handiwork. Who do you think came up with the idea of war, anyway?"

"Indeed," I interjected. "You mentioned the possibility of refreshments?" It had occurred to me that, if we were going to wander through the Kingdom of Death for who knew how long in search of my master, perhaps it would be better to eat first.

"Most certainly," our guide replied. "The food counter is in the back over there." He pointed to the rear of the building. I saw a small table, over which hung a placard which listed prices for "Rigor Mortis Burgers" and "Death Shakes." What kind of food was this?

"Uh," I added, for it occurred to me that I had seen no one but Devorno and Snarks within this building, "is there no one here to serve us?"

"Well, there may not be any*one* in particular," our guide explained a bit apologetically, "but there is definitely some*thing*." He pointed at the table in the back. "Simply put your money there, and state what it is that you desire. The item will appear almost instantaneously. It's a little disconcerting, I'll grant you. But around here, it's a lot more pleasant than many of the other possibilities. Trust me."

"Indeed," I replied. Now that I thought of it, I was wondering if I could trust the food. For one thing, there was something about the name "Rigor Mortis Burger" that did nothing for the appetite. And a second point to consider was Death's love for games. If the specter knew I was here, would it playfully add something to the burger that would ensure I would stay in Death's kingdom forever?

"On second thought," I stated, "I'm not hungry."

"Probably wise," Devorno admitted. "This place is worse than Slime-o-Rama."

"Home of the Slime Burgers?" Snarks responded. "That isn't possible!"

But the bus deity no longer heard the demon. Instead, he stared at the door through which we had entered, his face twisted in fright.

"I shouldn't have said that, should I?" he whimpered. "I know I'm under contract. Please, if you're going to— make it quick, and painless?"

A great shadow fell across the room. I wanted to turn

around, to confront the newcomer, but fear kept me rooted to the spot. Snarks, full of demonic bravery, wheeled about. His jaw opened in astonishment.

"It cannot be!"

A hand fell on my shoulder.

"Excuse me," said a voice both gentle and powerful. It was a voice I knew.

The newcomer spoke again:

"You wouldn't happen to know where I might find a wild pig?"

It was the Dealer of Death.

SIXTEEN

You can't go home again, and why would you want to, anyways?

—From *The Demonwise Guide to the Netherhells,
    or Why I'm Glad You're Going and I'm Not,*
        by Snarks,
most honest demon to ever come from down below
        (another tome still awaiting publication)

Snarks said what I could only think.

"What are *you* doing here?"

The Dealer of Death sighed. "That means you don't have any wild pigs, doesn't it?"

"Indeed," I replied. "I'm afraid we didn't think to bring any. But then we weren't expecting to encounter you, either."

The Dealer nodded. "You are no more surprised than I. One minute, I was facing up to that Netherhells committee, which was threatening to boil my blood. The next thing I knew, here I was—wherever this is."

I briefly answered that when I had last seen the Dealer, it had been in Vushta, after the demon committee had indeed boiled his blood, sending him into a near-death coma.

"Then he's dead?" Snarks asked in disbelief. "He doesn't look very dead to me."

"Nor do I feel it." The Dealer absently flexed his shoulder muscles as he considered my most recent statement. "And your explanation makes a great deal of sense to me, for it explains why I am different from the others here."

The large fellow cracked his knuckles, ten small, simultaneous explosions. "For although I am in this place, I do not seem subject to its rules in the same way as those I have met. Perhaps it is because my earthly body still straddles that line between life and death. From what I understand, Death usually takes a more active interest in cases like me who have halfway entered his kingdom. However, from what I have also heard, the specter has become obsessed with something lately, and has no time for the likes of me, instead spending its days muttering 'Eternal, eternal.' Whatever that means."

"Indeed," I said grimly. "I may have some idea."

The Dealer nodded happily. "I figured that you might. I've noticed that things always seem to happen around you, and decided that that was exactly what I needed. I mean, it's perfectly nice around here, except that perhaps it's a bit low-key. And I haven't strangled a single wild pig since I've gotten here!" He sighed again. "I mean, how can you strangle something when it's already dead?"

The Dealer's hands closed around an imaginary neck as he continued. "I shouldn't have hoped, I guess. It's simply when I saw you had a dragon outside, I thought . . ." His voice trailed off, leaving his fondest dream unsaid.

"Indeed?" I asked. "So you are here to help us?"

"Of course," the Dealer answered. "You're the sort of fellow who inspires that sort of thing."

I could do nothing but nod in return, for that very talent of mine was one of the reasons Death wanted me for its own. But I would not despair, for my master's life was in danger.

"Indeed," I began after I took a deep breath. "Then you will help me find the wizard Ebenezum?"

"Most certainly, if that is what you wish," the Dealer agreed. "It feels good to have a direction again. After all, an assassin in the land of the dead is a bit purposeless."

"Then lead on!" I pointed to the door. "Into the Kingdom of the Dead!"

"Wait a second!" Devorno interrupted. "What about the tour?"

"I am sorry, good guide," I responded, "but the tour will have to wait. We have a wizard to rescue and a world to save!"

"Hey, if you didn't like the tour, just say so!" the guide replied defensively. "Excuses, excuses, nothing but excuses."

"No, really!" I retorted, trying not to hurt the divinity's feelings. "We have to leave here, for reasons having nothing to do with you—"

"Sure, sure," the guide answered despondently. "Dig the knife in a little deeper. Why don't you tell me right out—"

"Okay," Snarks interrupted before I could further explain. "You found us out. I've never heard a more boring guide in my life. We didn't want to go on your tour, anyway! But now that we've left it, maybe we'll be able to wake ourselves up!"

"What?" Devorno replied in outrage. "Well, if that's the way you feel about it!"

The guide stormed past us out of the shop. A second later, I heard the strange sound that the bus made when it moved; then that sound, too, retreated into the distance.

Snarks nodded in satisfaction. "Cruel but fair. It's the demon way. Otherwise it would have taken us forever to get rid of him."

"Indeed," I said, wondering if there might have been some other way. But perhaps the demon was right for once, for now we were free to find my master.

I turned to the others, and told them there was no time to delay. Only, where could we begin?

"Leave that to me," the Dealer remarked quietly as he motioned us to follow him from the shop. "I have had time to explore, and I have found the perfect starting point."

Snarks and I accompanied the dealer outside the dwelling, where we found a somewhat disgruntled dragon.

"All I have to say," the reptile remarked sternly, "is, if you want the top of your bus back, you only have to ask." He paused to brush some imaginary dust from his tail. "Here I was, one minute basking in the glow of whatever it is the light around here comes from, and the next— whamo!—the bus has vanished and I am deposited on whatever passes for the ground around here, which is quite substantial, let me assure you." The dragon winced as he tried to sit. "What did you do to that deity? You guys didn't somehow incur his wrath or anything?"

I told the dragon I would explain everything as we moved. At the moment, the most important thing was to locate my master.

Hubert stared at the Dealer of Death.

"Say. Aren't you—"

The Dealer nodded.

"It doesn't surprise me," the dragon replied laconically. "Nothing surprises me anymore." He paused, then added hopefully: "I wonder if there's a song in there somewhere."

"Indeed," I added. "If only we had time to explore the possibilities. Unfortunately, we must follow the Dealer."

And we did just that, walking after the well-muscled assassin into that nearby forest that looked an awful lot like the Western Woods.

The Dealer frowned. "I know it's around here somewhere." He turned left, crossing a stream and passing a twisted oak that somehow seemed very familiar.

"Yes, yes!" the Dealer exclaimed with new excitement. "This is the way!"

I followed the assassin uneasily, almost overwhelmed by déjà vu. This was not simply the Western Woods; this was the corner of the woods directly behind Ebenezum's cottage.

"Ah!" the Dealer chortled. "As I suspected. Here we are."

And we were. We stepped out of the forest halfway between the cottage and the well from which I used to fetch water. But how could this be? We weren't in the Western Woods, we were in the Kingdom of Death.

"This is not the real thing," the Dealer assured me, "but an incredible simulation."

"But how would you know about this place?" I asked. "And how could you know that this looked like my master's cottage?"

"You forget," the Dealer replied, "that I am a member of the Urracht sect, the most fanatically devoted order of assassins that the world has ever known. When I was first hired by King Urfoo the Vengeful to kill your master and his companions, I, of course, spent a few days learning everything I could about the wizard. And that included all I could discover about the wizard's dwelling, should I have to kill him there. Now, certainly, that we are in the Kingdom of Death, all this killing business becomes academic. But still, it was important at the time."

"Indeed," I commented, impressed by this man's fanatical devotion. Thank goodness his mission to kill us was far in the past, or perhaps far in the future.

"So are we going to stand around here and admire the simulation," Snarks prompted, "or what?"

"Indeed, no," I replied. "But perhaps this place holds some clue to my master's whereabouts."

"It holds more than that." The dealer pointed at the steps that led into the cottage. "Look."

If I had been surprised before, now I was downright astonished, for on the top step was a very familiar pile of books and mystical instruments, a pile that had once resided in my pack, until I had been snatched aloft by a giant bird who wasn't too concerned about what happened to my possessions. And as I approached, I saw there were other things upon the pile as well: my stout oak staff, a hefty wizardry do-it-yourself book and the crystal ball.

"What is all this doing here?" I asked.

The Dealer considered. "These are all things that you lost, are they not?"

I nodded in wonder.

"Well," the Dealer continued, "here's where they are to be found. Perhaps all lost objects end in the Kingdom of the Dead, I don't know. Or perhaps this is a special case. Look around at this exact reproduction of your home in the

Western Woods. I told you before that I had studied you and your master. I have a feeling that someone, or something, else has become even more obsessed than I with where you and the wizard come from, so obsessed that it was forced to re-create all this, in hopes that it would give some clue as to your background, something that it could use to overcome its obsession. Am I correct?''

I nodded again. "The specter has done this, then, to seek out my weakness.''

The Dealer nodded in return. "Only time will tell if it has succeeded.''

"Indeed,'' I replied. "Then it is doubly important that I contact my master, for this strange place has given me the means to do so.''

I climbed the step and picked up the crystal ball, then paused a moment while I fished the incantation from my pocket. Would that Brownie never wake up? But I had no time to think of Tap now. I only had the time and energy to contact my master.

"Secret sphere, seashore seer—'' I began, rapidly reading through the rhyme without a hitch. The crystal ball clouded obediently, without errant noises or spoken messages. This time, it would work for sure!

"I must—'' I began, barely able to speak for the excitement rising within my breast. "I must speak with my master, the great wizard Ebenezum!''

To my astonishment, I was answered by a very familiar voice:

"Yes, Wuntvor?''

But I could see nothing in the crystal! I feared the clouds would keep me from fully contacting my master. I shook the sphere, trying to conquer the mystic forces therein.

"Master?'' I called. "Ebenezum? Where are you?''

Someone tapped me on the shoulder. I glanced around.

"Indeed,'' a voice intoned.

It was my master.

SEVENTEEN

"You ask if I have any comment about those six attractive and scantily clad women that were seen leaving my study the other day. And perhaps, because of that visit, it is true that I am not quite the wizard that you had thought me to be. Happily, however, the young women who visited me also had entirely different thoughts. Next question?"

—Ebenezum,
during the conference in which he claimed "that
everything about Wizardgate will be revealed"

"Indeed?" I cried, quite beside myself.

"Yes," my master replied. "Here I am. Death didn't know what else to do with me."

"Hey, that's great!" Hubert enthused. "Now that we've found the wizard, we can get out of here!" The dragon paused. "Uh, we *can* get out of here, can't we?"

"Indeed," my master said as he thoughtfully tugged on his beard. "How did you manage to find me in the first place? I imagine we could simply reverse the process."

"Oops," Snarks remarked as I glanced his way. "Hey, how could I know that boring tour guide might actually become important?"

I briefly described how we had enlisted Plaugg's aid to reach this place, but then had to somehow rid ourselves of the bus of the gods.

"I see," Ebenezum said when I was done. " 'Tis a shame, but it can't be helped. I am glad to see you, anyway, Wuntvor. Working together, we have a much better chance against the specter than I had by myself."

"So you can use magic around here?" Hubert asked.

"I suppose so. I don't seem to have the reaction to it I once had: sneezing and all that. However, there is a problem using magic in Death's domain. This house you see, these woods, the sky above us, the ground below, all are creations of the specter's imagination; of its own very powerful magic, if you will. Therefore, any spells you try here exist within that greater sorcery—Death's sorcery, perhaps the greatest magic ever known—which might give your own magic some unexpected results."

"Indeed," I replied, marveling at how well my master grasped the situation. It was good to be able to rely on his wisdom again.

"So, Wuntvor," the wizard asked, "what shall we do next?"

"In-indeed?" I stammered, rather taken aback. My master was here, and whenever I was with my master, he automatically took charge. At least that had happened until now. This time, however, he was asking for my advice!

I took a deep breath. Very well. My master's request had been a surprise, but I would not let it get the better of me. Ebenezum had been trapped in Death's kingdom for some time now, and perhaps felt his facilities were somewhat hampered by being so long in these surroundings. What more natural, then, but to ask advice of someone who was new on the scene, and not yet under the spell of the Kingdom of the Dead? It made perfect sense.

"Indeed," I repeated. "I had not given it much thought. I was so concerned with finding you that I had not spent much time planning what would happen thereafter. I do have a couple ideas, however."

"Indeed," the wizard mused, an odd glint in his eye. "You must share them with me."

"In a minute!" Snarks interjected. "First, the apprentice and I must have a conference."

"Really?" Ebenezum chuckled dryly. "I hardly think that is necessary."

"Indeed," I began, turning to the demon. "If there is some problem, cannot we all—"

"The necessity of our talk can only be determined as we confer," Snarks insisted. "Besides, it will only take a moment. You surely have a moment, after being here all this time."

"If you put it that way," I said, "I suppose—"

"Wuntvor!" my master barked, suddenly severe. "We are back together after all this time. Surely you don't need to leave now to talk to a demon?"

"Indeed," I replied. The wizard hardly sounded like himself. I guessed that the long days of being trapped in Death's domain had taken their toll. "Still, I don't think a minute—"

"Do not dispute me!" Ebenezum rumbled, his eyes dark with fury. "You will come with me now."

"But is that the wisest course?" I counseled the wizard. "I know that you must be anxious to leave this place, but until we fully consider the options—"

The wizard pointed at me with one long-fingered hand. "You will come with me now, or not at all."

"Very well," I answered, trying to calm my master down. "But are you sure this is the best way—"

"I know what the best course is for the Eternal Apprentice!" the mage exclaimed. "Wuntvor, take my hand!"

His long fingers reached for me, fingers that seemed bonier than I remembered. Had Death been starving my master as well? I glanced at Snarks, who was vehemently shaking his head. What did the demon know that he could not tell me? Surely, taking the wizard's hand could not harm me.

But I looked at that hand again, at those five bony, white fingers. Perhaps it would harm me, after all.

I took a step away.

"You will not get away that easily!" the mage declared

as he made a quick grab for me. I stepped aside, but his fingers gripped the flap of my pack, tearing it open.

"Eep eep!" cried the angry ferret as it erupted in the wizard's face.

"A ferret?" the mage shrieked. "Keep it away from me! You know how I feel about ferrets!"

Now I was sure something was wrong.

My master didn't feel one way or another about ferrets. The last time I had produced scores of them from my magic hat, he had taken them perfectly in stride. But I remembered something else that had an aversion to the small, rapidly reproducing creatures.

The mage brushed the animal aside and recomposed himself, staring at me with ever more hollow eyes.

"You will come with me now!" the wizard demanded, but somehow, silently, the Dealer had moved so that he stood between the mage and myself.

"Perhaps it is time to calm yourself," the Dealer said reasonably.

"Calm?" the wizard screamed. "How can I have any calm when *he* is here!" The mage's hand shook as he pointed at me. "I will have you yet!"

And with those words his robes changed, losing their silver moons and stars and becoming garments of darkest black. His hands turned bonier still, and the beard fell away, revealing a skull-like grin. Death's grin.

Death laughed, the sound of insects drowning in the incoming tide. "Why should I get upset? You are in my domain now. There is no way to escape." It spent a moment smoothing its robes; a moment, I suspect, used to gain the calm the specter already professed. "You have won our first little game. But there will be more; many more."

The death's-head smile seemed to widen. "I had wondered where you had gotten to. Heaven, was it? How very clever. But I should have expected something of the sort from the Eternal Apprentice! I was actually caught off my guard when you arrived, for at least half a minute." It laughed again, the sound of lemmings plunging to their doom. "Now, however, that we have been properly reintroduced, we shall play by my rules. You have no choice, if you ever want to see your master again!''

Death's laughter echoed about us, but the specter had vanished from our midst.

"Indeed," I said to Snarks, when I once again remembered to breathe. "Was that what you wished to tell me?"

"Something of the sort," the demon said. "It's a talent I picked up in the Netherhells. When you're surrounded by liars, cheats and confidence fiends from the day you are born, you tend to readily recognize the type. I wasn't exactly sure who that was at first. I was only certain that it was not your master. Then, I'll admit, when I guessed that it was really Death''—the demon shivered—''I was afraid if I went and told you about it the wrong way, we'd all get zapped.''

"I had no idea Death was such a great actor," Hubert added with new respect. "Imagine the career the specter could have if it wasn't so intent on killing people."

"We are in Death's kingdom," the Dealer reminded us quietly. "Here, the specter can do almost anything. Because we are still alive, it has no direct control over us. However, since this is its domain, I'm sure Death could devise any number of means to make us no longer alive."

"But if this being is so powerful," Snarks objected, "why are we still breathing?"

The Dealer nodded. "There is another factor we have not considered. Death seems to have an emotional problem when it comes to the Eternal apprentice—the mention of the name alone is enough to get the specter to lose its coldly rational head. When the Eternal Apprentice confronts it directly—well, then, death has *real* problems. And in those problems is the hope for our salvation."

"Indeed," I interjected, trying to comprehend the gist of what the Dealer had just told us. "I am quite impressed with your understanding of this situation."

"It is only natural, when you think about it," the Dealer replied humbly. "After all, as an assassin, death has been my life."

"Indeed," I said again. "But what you have told me is

disquieting as well. Death controls this kingdom so completely that it can make us see or feel anything it wishes."

"Within the limits I have already described," the Dealer agreed. "You can depend on nothing in this kingdom, except your wits."

"Indeed," I replied after a moment's consideration. "My wits?"

"His wits?" Snarks exclaimed. "Oh, no, we've lost for sure."

"No, not simply *his* wits," the Dealer reprimanded the demon. "Although you do make light of someone who is the Eternal Apprentice. But, besides his wits, we also have those of myself and the dragon. Not to mention *your* wits."

"Oh," Snarks said, a bit humbled. "My wits? In that case, we can't lose!"

"Indeed, we have more than those," I added. "For we also have the wits of the ferret, small as they may be, and two more intelligences as well."

I drew forth Cuthbert by way of demonstration.

"What? Huh?" the sword began. "I thought you were going to leave me in there forever! Oh, I know, sometimes I ask you to do things like that, but I don't really mean it. That is, I don't mean it as long as there's no blood to be spilled anywhere. There isn't, is there? Or ichor?"

I assured the talking blade that the immediate region was battle-free.

"Ah," Cuthbert sighed. "Then it's simply a chance to get free of my scabbard and see the sights. That's more like it! It's nice around here, too. Very bright and cheerful. Would anyone mind telling me where we are?"

I told the sword we were in the Kingdom of Death.

"The Kingdom of *what*?" Cuthbert squawked. "That does not sound at all positive. What are you going to want me to cut up around here? Trust you to find a place where there's something worse than ichor!"

"Alas," the Dealer of Death remarked. "Such is the lot of heroes."

"Oh-oh," the sword shuddered. "I remember *this* guy! When he was wielding me, it was blood city! Hack and slash, slash and hack, morning, noon and night. Then, for a change of pace, we did gorings and decapitations! This guy never paused for breath!''

"On the contrary," the Dealer interposed, "I find decapitations quite restful.''

"Indeed," I tried to calm the sword, for I, too, remembered when the Dealer had used Cuthbert to hack and slash his way across the Netherhells. "I imagine there will be scant need for killing, since everybody else around here is already dead. And, for similar reasons, I can't see any reason why I would have to lend you to someone.''

"That's the ticket!" Cuthbert cheered. "I'm your sword, and don't you forget it! Now, would you mind putting me back in my scabbard until we're someplace normal?''

I did as the sword requested.

"I'm not worried at all now," Snarks remarked. "That weapon is going to be a whole bunch of help!''

"But didn't you say there were *two* who could help us?" Hubert rumbled.

"That's true," I replied. "And I think it's time to wake the second one." I patted my pocket.

"The second one?" Snarks asked with a shudder. "In there?''

I nodded.

"You didn't bring—' the demon was unable to name the object of his fear.

I nodded again.

The demon looked up to the heavens, if there were indeed heavens in this realm.

"Is there no escape?" he whispered.

"Indeed," I said. "Not in this life." I tapped my pocket.

"Wha—" the Brownie mumbled. "Who?" The little fellow yawned and stretched, standing so that he could peer over the pocket top. "Sorry. I seem to have taken a little nap, there. Too much Brownie Power, I guess. Where are we? What time is it?''

A spectral laugh swallowed whatever answer I might have made. Death was once again in our midst.

"It is time for the games to begin," it intoned dryly.

I saw then that Death was not alone. It had brought a man-size cage along, and in that cage was my master, the wizard Ebenezum!

"These games will be different from those we've played before," Death continued summarily. "We are in my kingdom, so we will play by my rules. It goes without saying, of course, that I also get to choose the games we play."

"Indeed—" I began.

"An interesting point," Death conceded before I could go any further. "In the sake of fairness, therefore, for I may be more experienced at one or two of these pastimes, I suggest we play best out of three. Any objections?"

"Indeed—" I tried again.

"Excellent," the specter replied. "As in any true game, there is of course a prize for winning, and a forfeit for losing. The prize, you will be happy to learn, is the wizard Ebenezum, as well as freedom for you and your companions. That was what you were going to ask, wasn't it?"

"Indeed," I answered, "but—"

"Oh, yes," Death hurriedly added, "if you win and are returned to the world you know, you will of course be allowed to live out the rest of your natural lives." The specter grinned at each of us. "However long or short those lives may be."

"Indeed!" I interjected once more. "However—"

"Oh, the forfeit!" Death chuckled, the sound of a fish flopping about in a bucket as it drowns in the open air. "Well, you know what that is, don't you? If you lose two, none of you get to leave. And the Eternal Apprentice is mine forever!"

I was silent this time.

"Do you accept?" Death demanded.

What could I do? I looked over at my master. He solemnly nodded back at me. Did that mean I should accept Death's challenge? What other way could I possibly have of rescuing the wizard and escaping the specter's clutches?

There was only one answer.

"Indeed," I replied.

"Excellent!" Death said heartily. The specter swept back its robes and surveyed me and all my companions before it spoke again. "I have thought upon this moment long and hard, and I have decided that for our first game, we should have something steeped in tradition. A game of skill, and a game of champions. And only one game could truly suit all these criteria."

Death raised his hand, palm up, before him, and in that hand appeared a sphere not unlike my crystal ball, save that this new globe was jet-black.

"The game, gentlemen"—Death spoke slowly, drawing out the suspense—"is bowling."

EIGHTEEN

There are rumors that I have heard that wizards are not "good sports." Nothing could be further from the truth. Most mages I know will be glad to turn you into any number of lower animals and other life-forms. What? You don't want to be turned into a tadpole or tree fungus? Well, who's being a good sport now? No answer, huh? Oh, I forgot, tree fungi can't talk. Can they?"

—Introductory chapter to the great wizard Ebenezum's
newest self-help course,
How to Make Friends and Influence People by Threatening to Turn Them Into Toads,
never released to the general public,
due to some problems among test groups with getting
tree fungi to continue paying for lessons

"B-bowling?" I sputtered. "But we have never heard of such a thing!"

Death waved away my objections with a bony hand. "You will pick it up soon enough. If not"—it paused to stare at me with its blank eye sockets—"perhaps we can give you all of eternity to practice."

The specter waved both hands. "But I said this was a

159

game of champions.'' The hands pointed to his right. ''Therefore, let my champion appear.''

A puff of orange smoke appeared where Death had indicated, and there stood a man, average-looking, a couple inches shorter than myself, fairly well muscled, but no match for a specimen like the Dealer of Death. All in all, the fellow looked absolutely too ordinary to be a champion, save for one thing: his bright orange and green shirt. I looked more closely at this strange new garment, and saw that over the pocket was written a single word: ''Ernie.''

''This is my champion,'' Death announced as it waved its hands again. ''And this is our field of battle.''

A long wooden aisle appeared before us, at the end of which stood ten clublike objects.

''Ernie?'' Death said to his champion. ''If you would explain?''

''Gladly.'' The champion nodded pleasantly to the rest of us. ''How you doin', fellas?'' He picked up the black sphere, which had reappeared by the wooden aisle. ''This is a bowling ball. That''—he nodded at the aisle—''is the lane, down which you roll the ball. The object of the game is to hit those pins''—he pointed at the club things at the other end—''and knock them over. Every time it's your turn, you get two tries to knock the pins down. The more pins you knock down, the better you do. Like this.''

Ernie took three steps forward and launched the ball down the wooden lane. The ball curved slightly, then swung back in again, knocking all ten pins over with a solid crash.

''That, gentlemen,'' Ernie continued, ''is the best you can do. It's known as a strike. If you take both your turns to knock down all the pins, it's known as a spare. You'll get extra points—''

''Enough explanations!'' Death interrupted. ''They can ask questions as they go along. I've waited too long for this to delay another instant! They must choose their champion now!''

''Indeed,'' I replied. ''If you—''

''Ah,'' Death answered before I could go further. ''You would like some privacy? Of course.''

I didn't feel any movement, nor did I see Death, his champion and the caged Ebenezum move, yet, somehow, there were now a hundred yards between us. It was all a bit disconcerting. Still, it was no more disconcerting than Death answering me before I had spoken. I would have to deal with it somehow. But why didn't I feel more positive about that thought?

"Indeed," I said to my companions. "We need a champion."

"For bowling?" Snarks despaired.

"If you could distract those guys," Hubert offered, "I might be able to knock the pins down with my tail."

"And I might be able to influence the ball with Brownie Power," Tap piped up. "However, it would be much better if the game had shoes in it."

"No," I replied, "I have the feeling that if we tried to influence the game through magical means, Death would simply influence it the other way. We will play honestly, unless Death does otherwise. And I think there is only one here with the skill and accuracy necessary to become our champion, to stand up in the face of Death and overcome any challenge—"

"I'm touched by this show of faith—" Hubert began.

"No, no," I gently told the dragon. "Your expertise lies in other, more theatrical areas. For the sport of bowling, I'm afraid we must turn to the Dealer."

"I shall do my best," the assassin replied humbly. "Perhaps I can imagine that the ball is a wild pig."

I clapped the well-muscled fellow on the shoulder, hurting my hand slightly. "I'm sure you will do admirably," I said as I flexed my hand behind my back.

"You are decided?" Death asked, suddenly at our side once more. "Good! Let the competition begin!" The specter coughed delicately. "I, of course, will act as commentator."

Somehow, the light around us dimmed, so that the only truly bright spot was in the vicinity of the bowling lane. I heard the soft murmur of a crowd. Death apparently had seen fit to bring some of its ghosts along.

"Your champion should go first," the Dealer declared. "I need to study his form."

"Very good," Death repeated in a strangely hushed tone. "The challenger has elected for our Bowling for Souls champion to start. Ernie waits for the pins to set. He takes careful aim. One, two, three steps, and a perfect release! The ball's rolling, rolling. It looks good! Yes, it's a strike!"

The ball had hit the first pin ever so slightly to one side, which helped knock over the pins behind it, and they the pins behind them. All ten were down. It was an impressive performance. Was there any way the Dealer could match it?

The assassin looked grimly down the lane as the pins magically righted themselves.

"I will do my best," he whispered to me. "No less could be expected from one of the Urracht!"

He held the ball as he saw the champion hold it, and took the same steps, one, two, three.

"Now the challenger has the ball," Death's soft voice intoned. "He steps forward cautiously."

Something squealed out in the audience.

"The challenger releases the ball," Death announced. "Uh-oh, it's curving the wrong way. It looks like a gutter ball!"

The Dealer stared out into the audience. "Is that a wild pig?"

"The challenger receives a second ball," Death droned on.

"I could have sworn I heard a wild pig," the Dealer insisted.

"The challenger must release the ball, or forfeit his turn," Death replied with no change of tone.

"That's the way it's going to be, then?" the assassin remarked grimly. "So be it."

"The challenger gets the ball, and prepares himself again," Death returned to describing the action. "Here comes the approach."

This time the squeal was even louder. The Dealer barely flinched.

"There goes the ball. It looks like a better shot this time. He'll at least get a couple pins. No! It's curving in! Give five, no, six pins to the challenger."

His turn completed, the Dealer silently returned to my side. He whispered in my ear:

"You do not toy with the Urracht!"

"The champion once again has the ball," Death commented.

Ernie glanced nervously at the specter.

"Isn't it getting a little noisy in here?"

The champion was right. Not only were there wild-pig noises out there, but the crowd was getting louder as well. Another ploy, I imagined, to undermine the Dealer's confidence. Now, however, that the assassin knew about these tricks, I felt Death might be in for a surprise.

"The champion is being a bit temperamental," Death replied. "He has obviously forgotten what happens in this kingdom to temperamental champions. But no, now he is steeling himself, reaching inside for that special something shared by all great athletes. He moves forward with the ball. There it goes. It looks good—maybe just a little off. Oh, too bad! Five pins down. The shot was a bit too much to the right side."

Ernie waited for the ball to come back to him. He had begun to sweat, even though the air wasn't appreciably warm. I wondered exactly *what* it was that they did to temperamental champions down here.

"Here he goes again," Death whispered. "Yes, he's got it! The other five are down! That's Ernie for you! He always gives a hundred and ten percent. What a competitor!"

It was the Dealer's turn again, but this time he approached with a determination that went beyond anything I had ever seen before, a fanaticism based on the total destruction of ten pins at the far end of the lane.

The assassin felled all ten with the first ball, despite the three wild-pig bleats from the audience.

"An impressive move," Death muttered, "but it won't phase the champion."

Ernie, however, looked completely phased. His hair was matted now with sweat, and he jumped every time something made a sound like a wild pig.

"I-I am not used to w-working under these conditions!" he stammered.

"Some champions may get used to not working at all," Death replied. The threat did little good. Ernie got two pins with his first ball, and only one with his second.

The Dealer got another strike, despite a full score of wild pigs crying their hearts out.

He nodded grimly to me upon his return.

"Before, it was just a ball and ten pins. Now it is a weapon against ten wild pigs!"

We would win this one. The Dealer of Death was in his element.

"Okay, okay!" Death remarked in a more normal tone. "I know when I'm beaten. I forfeit. You win the first of the three challenges."

Hubert cheered as Ernie disappeared.

"But perhaps it was a bit unfair," Death continued generously, "presenting you with a sport that you had never witnessed before as your first game. I think the next contest shall be a bit simpler—say, a guessing game?"

"A contest of wits?" Snarks demanded. "Let's have at it, then. I am ready."

"As I knew you would be. But we are not quite prepared. Give me a moment while I call up an impartial third party."

There was a puff of blue smoke by Death's left side, quickly replaced by a tall, frail fellow with stooped shoulders and squinting eyes.

"Our judge," Death introduced the newcomer.

"I'm as impartial as they get in this kingdom," the frail fellow agreed.

"And I have appointed our judge as keeper of the rules," the specter added. "I trust that is satisfactory?"

"Indeed," I replied, not wishing to quibble over a minor point. "And what rules must we follow?"

The judge unfolded a crumpled sheet of parchment. His voice quavered slightly as he read:

"The first rule is that no one is to ask about the rules. The penalty is an immediate forfeit."

"What?" Snarks demanded. "How can we forfeit a game we don't even know about?"

"It is a little severe, so early in the game," Death agreed. "Why don't we give them another chance?"

"You're the boss," the frail fellow replied. "The game goes on."

"I should say so!" Snarks exclaimed. "Who ever heard of those kinds of rules!"

The judge further unfolded the parchment before him, and again read aloud:

"The second rule is that no one is to complain about the rules. The penalty is immediate forfeit."

"Wait a second!" Snarks demanded. "That rule is all tied up with the first one. This is no fair at all!"

"I'm sorry," the judge replied, "but it says here—"

"Now, now," Death interrupted. "Even I will admit that these rules are a bit arbitrary. Why not give our guests one more chance? That way, no one could possibly accuse us of any bias."

The judge shrugged. "If you say so." He nodded to the rest of us. "You guys are getting off easy here. The game goes on again. Well?" He tapped his foot impatiently. "It's your move!"

Snarks turned to me. "What do we do?"

"Indeed," I replied, for I had given the matter some thought. "We do nothing."

"Nothing?" the demon replied.

"Exactly. For what has happened the last two times we attempted to start the game?"

"We immediately lost." Snarks's face brightened as he saw my point. "Oh, I see! You're saying that the game is so constructed that if you attempt to play it—"

"You lose," I finished the thought for him. "So the only thing we can do—the only way we can win—is if we refuse to play."

"Brilliant!" Snarks admitted. "And coming from a human, too! My hat would be off to you, if I wore one."

"So," the judge called to us. "What is the delay? The game must continue!"

I cautioned my companions to silence with a single glance.

"No response?" the judge frowned. "I see." He further unfolded his parchment and read:

"The third rule is that, should anyone refuse to continue playing the game, they will automatically lose. In other words, immediate forfeit."

This time Death shrugged. "What else can we do? I think the judge and I have been more than fair."

"The game is over," the judge agreed.

Death tsked. "Unfortunately, you have brought this upon yourselves, gentle beings, and you have lost. We now stand tied with one contest apiece."

The judge popped out of existence, and the specter paused a moment to stare at each of us in turn.

"I think we should all take a few minutes," Death said slowly, "and consider the importance of our last contest, which will be far more trying than either of those which have gone before. After all, the third game decides whether the wizard goes back with you, or you come to me, for all eternity."

Death's laugh was so cold that it seemed to freeze my heart.

And his laughter went on forever.

NINETEEN

Sometimes, being in the magic business can be a little difficult. Then again, sometimes it can be down-right dangerous. In fact, in certain situations, this kind of work can become outright deadly. And then there's times when it gets really bad—

—Unfinished chapter from *Some Thoughts
on Apprenticeship,*
by Wuntvor, apprentice to Ebenezum,
greatest wizard in the Western Kingdoms
(a work in progress)

"The time is come!"

Death once again stood at arm's reach.

I shook my head. Before this last contest began, there was one more deceit that needed to be taken care of.

"Indeed!" I called to the specter, for I would not lose this battle without a fight. "Before we begin our last contest, I need a promise."

"A promise?" The fiend nodded its bony head. "Very well. As you know, Death always keeps its promises."

"Good," I replied. "Then show us the real Ebenezum."

The specter chuckled. "Oh, you want to see the *real* wizard! I suppose, if you insist—"

167

Death waved its hands, and the mage within the cage changed subtly. The revised wizard pulled at his robes as he looked about.

"Why, Wuntvor," my master remarked. "What are you doing here?"

"I have come to save you!" I replied.

"Indeed?" The mage tugged reflectively at his beard. "I am a little hazy on exactly where I am. However, your mission sounds like a laudable goal, at the very least."

Snarks tugged at my shirt. "How did you know?"

"Indeed," I answered. "Once you had alerted me to Death's initial deception, it was simplicity itself. Until a moment ago, the magician in the cage had been too still, too silent. In short, he had not acted at all like my master. It was another of Death's ploys, designed, I am sure, like the wild-pig squeals during the first contest, to hurt us through surprise."

"You are too clever for me, Eternal Apprentice!" Death hissed. "but it will not matter, for our last battle is not one of wits, but of wills."

The specter stepped even closer to me. "Gaze into my eyes, you who are called Wuntvor—in this life. For our last test shall be a staring contest! It is simplicity itself— whoever looks away first, loses. And the contest begins now!"

I looked up and found myself gazing into the twin eye sockets of Death, two pools of blackness so deep that you might fall into them forever. I wanted to look away, before I lost my soul somewhere in those deep recesses. But I could not, no matter how my instincts screamed for escape for, the moment my gaze shifted, then truly would I be lost for eternity. I was forced to gaze into the void, deeper and deeper into a darkness that was never-ending. And, somehow, I had to stare into Death's gaze long enough to overcome this supernatural being. I had to do it for my soul, for my companions, for my master!

"Stare," Death prompted with a laugh, the sound of small beetles roasting to death beneath the desert sun. "Stare deep, Eternal Apprentice."

I was surrounded by blackness, a total absence of light

that went on forever, before me and to either side and, I was sure, behind me as well. I was surrounded by Death's darkness. I felt panic rise within me. What was happening? Was I trapped within the specter's stare? Would I be lost in it as well?

Then Death spoke again:

"Stare forever, Eternal Apprentice."

And its voice broke the spell. For why did Death want me? Because I *was* the Eternal Apprentice? And did not Death desire my soul because it had been—until this moment—forever beyond the specter's grasp? Death was not my master! In a way, if what the specter said about me was true, we were equals, the fiend always taking life, while I returned to it over and over again. And if we were equals, there was no reason to panic, no reason, indeed, to doubt that I might be able to win this contest.

"Indeed," I replied to the specter, and as soon as I had spoken, my perspective changed, and I was no longer lost deep within the fiend's gaze, but was instead staring once again at the skull-face of Death.

The specter's never-ending smile twitched unpleasantly.

"You fight me, apprentice. Don't you know that you have already lost? Don't you know that, sooner or later, everybody loses to Death?"

This time, I laughed. Death had tried to intimidate me with the force of its presence. Well, perhaps two could travel that road.

"Is that so?" I answered. "Then how do you explain my existence?"

"Then you admit it!" Death screamed triumphantly. "You admit you are the Eternal Apprentice! Oh, how sweet the victory will be, now that I know you are truly the one I seek!"

Oh, dear, I thought. This was not necessarily the result I was looking for. Death's smile reasserted itself, as if the specter was ready now to squander even the last ounce of its energy to defeat me.

"You will look away, Eternal Apprentice," Death whispered, "and you will lose."

It was then that I heard the ghosts. Faintly at first, but

stronger with every passing second—the clank of armor, the shouts of men, the tread of mailed boots across packed earth. The noise grew louder still, until it was almost deafening. And it came from everywhere, as if we were being surrounded by an army that went on forever.

"Wuntvor!" Hubert called. "We are being attacked!"

"Indeed!" I yelled back at the dragon, for I could not look away. "You must hold them off, for the sake of my master, and all our souls!"

I heard the clank of ghostly swords and shields, but then I heard more: the roar and crackle of Hubert's flame, the sharp thwack of Snarks's staff, the near-silent blows of the Dealer and the rapidly dancing feet of the Brownie. They would keep my back and flanks safe from these marauding spirits. Together, my companions would hold them until we had won!

But even as I stared at those bottomless eye sockets before me, I could see other things moving in the corners of my vision. I realized then, with a grim certainty, that the ghosts were not content to merely attack my fellows, but were advancing around Death as well, a legion headed straight for me. I caught a glimpse of a spectral sword. Another of the haunted horde flashed a red dagger that I hoped was covered with ghostly blood.

Could I be harmed by ghosts? I feared the answer, and I would know all too soon, for they would be upon me in an instant. Still, they were not unstoppable. From what I heard, my fellows were taking care of any number of the ghostly warriors. But how could I fend them off without looking away from Death?

And then it occurred to me: Perhaps I could not, but my weapon could.

I drew my trusted sword.

"Eek!" Cuthbert shrieked. "What's going on here? This doesn't look at all good! Listen! I take back what I said about getting out of my scabbard from time to—"

"Indeed," I said, interrupting the sword's hysteria. "I am sorry, but you must fight, perhaps harder than you ever have before."

"This is sounding worse with every passing minute!" Cuthbert complained. "Don't I have any say in this matter?"

"Indeed," I answered. "You could completely refuse to do my bidding."

"Really?" the sword replied, calming a bit. "Say, that's awfully nice of you."

"Of course," I continued, "then I would most likely be murdered by these marauding ghosts."

"Gee," Cuthbert remarked uncertainly. "Do you think so?"

"I can't see it going any other way." I paused for a second, then mused, "Of course, there's nothing for you to worry about. No matter what happens to me, there's no chance at all of you being abandoned. The moment I am dead, I'm sure the Dealer will scoop you up and get to work."

"The Dealer? You mean old hack-and-slash?" the sword asked distastefully. "Do you really think so?"

"Well," I replied, "look at it this way: Who's going to stop him?"

"Oh—er—who ever said I didn't want to fight? I'm your sword forever!" Cuthbert cheered. "Onward, into the fray!"

The sword had made its decision not a moment too soon, for the fray, as it were, was coming to us, the legion of ghosts moaning forward to the attack.

"You have to defend yourself, Eternal Apprentice," Death leered. "You have to look away!"

I laughed with a bravado that I almost felt, for Cuthbert guided my hand as I continued to stare deep within Death's dark orbs. I heard the ghostly clang of my sword against whatever it was it fought.

"I think not," I answered the specter. "It takes more than a few pitiful ghosts to defeat the likes of me!"

"Few?" Death sputtered. "Pitiful?" The specter almost glanced away to look at its legions. Almost, but not quite. For the first time, I realized I had a real chance of defeating this creature. The Dealer had said Death had a problem with me. Perhaps I could make that problem the specter's undoing.

"Hah!" my sword cried triumphantly. "Got you!"

I heard another sound, half slice, half gush, like an axe cutting through week-old snow.

"Oh, no!" Cuthbert moaned. "There is something worse than ichor! Ectoplasm!"

"I've gone altogether too easy on you, so far!" Death screamed at me, far more overwrought than the situation warranted. "We'll see how eternal you are, after you've faced my berserker legion!"

"Berserker legion?" Cuthbert asked uncertainly. "I do not like the sound of that!"

I didn't like the sound of what came next, either, for the ghostly moaning about us rose, becoming an unearthly shriek that seemed to have no end.

"Good," the Dealer stated calmly from somewhere nearby. "At last I will have a challenge."

"Look at these guys!" Snarks wailed, and for once, I was glad I could not.

The shrieking was joined by a rhythmic clanking, as if spectral swords clanged against ghostly shields, first ten, then a hundred, then five hundred strong.

"I think it's time for reinforcements!" Snarks screamed.

"Do you mean—" I called back.

"Plaugg!" Snarks replied. "O most unexceptional of deities, we beseech you! We need your barely tolerable aid, and we need it now!"

There was nothing for a moment, but then there was a voice, very faint but somehow still clearly understandable despite the wailing ghosts.

"I hear you, my worshipper."

"Oh, Your Adequateness!" Snarks yelled. "We need you here at once!"

"Oh, dear," the deity's faint voice replied. "How can I put this? You see"—Plaugg coughed distantly—"I'm afraid that is impossible."

"Impossible?" the demon wailed. "But why, Your Pretty-Goodness?"

"The driver refuses to go on that route again," Plaugg explained, his voice fainter with every word. "Something about a bus full of insulting travelers—"

And then Plaugg's voice was gone.

"Oh, no," Snarks murmured. "Have I doomed us all?"

But I could not believe this was the end. I was so close to saving my master. There had to be a way!

"Wuntvor!" a voice called to me above the ghostly chaos. My master's voice!

"Indeed?" I called back, my eyes still fixed on the specter.

"If you allow Death to attack you over and over again, you will lose!" the wizard exclaimed. "You must form a counterattack!"

"Silence, pitiful mage!" Death barked. "You are still under my control!"

"Is he?" I shot back at the specter. "I do not think he will be for long."

For a thought had occurred to me. My master had said we needed a weapon for a counterattack. But what better weapon was there than my master, the great wizard Ebenezum?

At first, I thought our magic was useless in Death's domain. But Snarks had somehow managed to call Plaugg. And the Brownie seemed to be holding his own against the ghostly warriors, for I was sure, could I but turn my head, that I would see shoes raining from nowhere upon our enemy. Therefore, Brownie magic worked here. And who had told us that it wouldn't? Not Ebenezum, but Death, disguised as the wizard.

Ah, but that specter was clever. And I had to be more clever still, if the Eternal Apprentice was to win the day.

"Snarks!" I called to the demon. "I need your help!"

"I've been—telling you that—ever since we've met!" Snarks yelled back between blows of his stout oak staff.

"Indeed," I answered. "I need you to get something out of my pack."

"I'd be—glad to," Snarks replied. "Soon as I—can get away."

"Tap! Hubert! Dealer!" I called to the others. "I need your aid as well. You must form a semicircle behind me, to protect Snarks while he does my bidding."

"Brownie Power to the rescue!" Tap announced.

Hubert assured me: "My most dramatic flame is in your service."

"I find any strategic move fascinating," the Dealer added.

"Okay, boss man!" Snarks interjected. "The demon wit is at your service!"

Look inside my pack," I instructed him. "There you will find a book—a Home Study Course."

I heard a rustling at my back.

"Eep! Eep eep eep!"

Snarks yelped. "Can't you do *something* about that ferret?"

"Sorry," I apologized. "But my guess is that the ferret can take care of itself."

"A ferret?" Death screamed his distaste. "You dare to bring a ferret into this battle?"

The specter wavered, almost looking away again. If *I* made him nervous, my ferrets made him doubly so.

"Magic for the Millions?" Snarks read as he retrieved the book.

"That's the one," I assured him. "Now, look in the back, under multiplication spells."

I heard the sound of pages turning.

"Don't you dare let that ferret get near me!" Death warned. But the specter calmed itself as soon as it spoke. "But what am I saying? I am Death. And Death always wins." The fiend chuckled aridly. "No mere ferret can save you now!"

"Multiplication spells?" Snarks mused. "Oh, there's a lot of them. In fact, there may be a few too many! Would you mind telling me what you'd like to multiply?"

"Shoes," I replied. "At least at first."

The Brownie cheered as Snarks asked if I was kidding.

"Indeed, no," I replied. "We need to quickly reproduce something to keep these ghosts away. Thanks to the Brownie, we already have a rain of footwear. Why not increase it?"

"And do it soon, would you?" Cuthbert pleaded. "The ghosts are everywhere. There's a whole lot of cutting going on here."

"I think a general multiplication spell is best," I further informed the demon, "for we will have to use it on something else later."

"One general spell coming up!" I once again heard Snarks flipping pages.

"Blechh! Blechh! Bllecchh!" the sword screamed. "Ectoplasm is cold! Ectoplasm is slimy! Ectoplasm is everywhere!"

"Ah, here we go!" the demon said triumphantly. "A multiplication spell, short and simple. How do you want to do it?"

"Indeed," I answered, careful to keep my gaze locked on that of Death while my sword hand leaped about under Cuthbert's guidance. "I fear that spell casting is beyond me at the moment. I'm afraid that the honor of making magic must pass to you."

"Me?" Snarks squealed in disbelief. "But I'm a demon. Wizards are supposed to cast spells on demons, not the other way around. I mean, there are certain proprieties—"

"And if we follow them, we shall be killed," I interrupted. "Still, I can see your point. I suppose if a demon isn't good enough to perform magic—"

"N-not good enough—I never said anything of the kind!" Snarks retorted. "Demons may come from the bottom, but they rate way on top! I will perform magic that will put Brownie Power to shame! Now, if the rest of you will look the other way, while I make a fool of myself trying to get this spell to work—"

The rest of us were too busy fighting off our ghosts to reply.

"You make such foolish plans," Death chuckled. "Why not surrender now, before I make you look ridiculous throughout eternity?"

"Indeed," I said sharply as I heard Snarks shuffling through the spell behind me. "The Eternal Apprentice is free to be ridiculous anytime he chooses! If I have my way, you will never have any control over that!"

Snarks called out strings of arcane words while clapping his hands and whistling. He hooted like an owl three times, yelled loudly and did something complicated with his feet upon the packed ground.

"The shoes!" Tap called. "The shoes are coming!"

A chorus of ghostly cries rose around us. I heard an "Ouch!" here, a "Yelp!" there, an "Oh, no, not high heels!" somewhere else.

"They are falling back!" the Dealer announced. "Your plan worked."

"Of course it did," Snarks agreed. "Wasn't there a demon involved—ow!"

I felt it, too. The shoes were not only falling on the ghosts. Now they were dropping on us as well. It began as an occasional soft-soled sandal, but I could hear boots dropping in my vicinity. Soon, the rain of shoes would make us helpless as well.

There was only one person I knew that could stop this sort of thing. Now that the ghosts had retreated, it was time to free him.

"Hubert!" I shouted over the ever-increasing thump-thump-thump of cascading footwear. "Dealer! We have to get Ebenezum out of this cage!"

Death laughed, still only flinching slightly beneath the shoe rain.

"Free your master? Whatever makes you think I will allow that?"

"You will have no choice!" I replied. "Snarks, now that you have mastered the spell to multiply shoes, it is time to turn it to other purposes. It is time to multiply ferrets!"

"Ferrets?" Snarks quavered. "He wanted me, a demon, to cast a spell. Well, I'm adaptable, especially in situations of life and death. And then he wanted the spell to produce shoes! Now, now, I calmed myself, it is life and death, after all, and it will probably be the most distasteful task you ever will have to perform. I mean, what could be worse than shoes? And then he tells me!" The demon choked, the next word lodged in his throat. "F-f-ferrets!"

This was too much. There was no longer any time for Snarks's objections. But could I trust the shoes to continue to keep the ghosts at bay? Careful not to take my eyes away from Death, I ran quickly to the demon's side. There was but one thing to do.

"Here," I said, handing the demon my sword.

"Huh?" Snarks replied.

"What?" Cuthbert yelped.

"If you don't want to cast, you've got to cut!" I answered the demon. "Now, quickly, repeat the spell to me, and I shall perform it!"

"What?" Cuthbert yelped again.

I managed to pat the sword's hilt as I finally released it into the demon's grip. "Now, now," I said reassuringly for Cuthbert's benefit. "You'll just keep on doing that fine job." My now free hand waved absently in the direction of the Dealer of Death. "Unless, of course, you'd rather I gave you to somebody else."

"I'm cutting!" Cuthbert shrieked. "I'm cutting!"

"Indeed," I murmured. "Now, Snarks, repeat the directions for the spell."

"Do I have to?" the demon whined.

"You could cast it yourself," I suggested.

"You convinced me," Snarks said. "You want me to start now?"

"In a moment," I replied, making sure that my gaze was firmly interlocked with that of Death. I had managed for some time to meet the specter's stare, and, apart from a slight watering in the corners of my eyes, was none the worse for wear. If I could simply concentrate on the spell while continuing to stare at Death, I could not help but succeed. And what problems could I have? Snarks, a rank beginner at the art of magic, had managed the multiplication spell to perfection. It should therefore be no problem at all for one with my experience. So why was I worried? Nothing could stop us now!

I took a deep breath.

"Begin."

"If that's the way you want it," Snarks agreed, and began to relay the spell to me.

"You will not stop me with your ferrets!" Death screamed, although there seemed to be a bit of panic in the specter's tone.

I told Snarks to ignore the fiend. In turn, the demon told me to clap, and I clapped. He told me to whistle, and I whistled. He told me to give three owl hoots, and I did that as well.

"Uh-oh," Snarks mumbled mid-spell. "Here come the ghosts."

"One ferret or a hundred ferrets!" Death proclaimed, cheered by its advancing army. "It makes no difference. I will not be stopped by those small, insignificant creatures, no matter how lively they may be." Still, if the specter was so sure of itself, why did its voice crack?

"Now here—comes the—difficult part," Snarks managed, fending off renewed attacks from the ghostly horde. "You must step left, jump, shuffle, step right, shuffle and jump. Quickly now!"

I did as the demon instructed, stepping, then jumping.

"It will never work, Eternal Apprentice," Death insisted. "I no longer feel any fear of your little helpers!"

Perhaps it was Death's repeated taunts that unnerved me. Or perhaps it was merely trying to concentrate simultaneously on Death's stare and my dancing feet. Whatever, when I attempted my second shuffle, I slipped and almost fell, barely managing to keep my gaze locked with that of the specter. It was more difficult than I realized to shuffle when you could not glance at your feet. But I had to finish the spell, and trust that my slight misstep would not change the outcome.

I stepped and jumped and shuffled. Come, ferrets! I thought. Perhaps they would not turn the tide for good, as Death had claimed, but at the very least they would distract the specter long enough for me to think of something else.

"Eep!" my ferret cried. I took the small animal's cry as a good sign. The spell must be working.

"Snarks!" I called. "Are the ferrets multiplying?"

"Eep!" The ferret screamed somewhat more insistently.

"Well," Snarks admitted, an odd tone to his voice, "not exactly."

And at that moment, the ground I stood upon was shaken by a thunderous cry:

"EEEP!"

"What?" Death whispered. "It cannot be!"

"EEEP!" the deafening sound came again, whatever made it saying, "Yes, it very well *can* be."

"No, not that large," Death groaned. "I could deal with anything—anything but something like that—anything but a fifty-foot ferret!"

And then the ground shook of its own accord. The ferret was coming.

"EEEP!"

"No," Death whispered. "I won't allow it! Not in *my* kingdom!"

It was too much for the specter, too much eeping life for it to even comprehend. It hugged its robes close by its sides, trying to shrink away from the approaching behemoth, the stupendous gray form moving inexorably toward it through the falling shoes.

"No!" Death shrieked. "Anything but *that* ferret!"

And then a great, furry shadow fell across the specter.

"EEEP!"

Death shrieked, looking up and away, searching for some escape from the rapidly descending ferret.

Death had looked away. I had won.

"Indeed," Ebenezum remarked from close by my side. "This might be a good time for a change of scene."

TWENTY

"Very well. If I must, I will fully explain every-thing. Let me begin with a demonstration. What am I doing? Only a very simple spell of forgetfulness. What spell of forgetfulness, you ask? Does anyone remember what I was talking about? What are you all doing here, anyways?"

—Ebenezum's final comments on Wizardgate, whatever that was

"Indeed, yes," I replied. "Do you have any idea how we might leave?"

"No problem at all," my master assured me. "This sojourn in the Kingdom of Death seems to have com-pletely cured my malady. My guess is that, in a place like this, one goes beyond sneezing."

"You're not going anywhere!" Death screamed hysteri-cally as it rapidly retreated. "I'll deal with you, as soon as I'm finished with this—animal!"

"I'm afraid not," I replied to the specter as my master assumed standard conjuring position. "After all, I won."

"Won?" Death hyperventilated, upset perhaps by how easily the huge ferret galloped after it. "Well, I suppose you did, technically. However, I'm quite certain ferrets are against the rules!"

"Rules?" Snarks asked. "What rules?"

"Indeed," Ebenezum interrupted. "If you fellows would gather around me, we'll be leaving now."

"All right, so you've won!" Death screamed as it ran from the monstrous rodent. "Enjoy the rest of your lives, as pitifully short as they will be! I'll be seeing you!"

"Indeed," I replied. "Will you?"

The specter's unearthly shriek was caught short by my master's spell.

All was darkness, then all was light.

I opened my eyes when someone said "Doom." We were back in Vushta, surrounded by wizards and companions. The wizards, as usual, were sneezing.

"Over?" Cuthbert shrieked, still a bit hysterical. "It's really over?" The sword whistled with relief. "Say, would anybody know anything about getting rid of dried ectoplasm stains?"

"Later," I said to the sword as I reclaimed and resheathed it.

"Indeed," Ebenezum called to the others. "Were you expecting us?"

"Doom, no," Hendrek answered. "We were expecting what you landed on top of."

"EEEP!" the fifty-foot ferret who had returned with us remarked.

"What? Who?" an old woman's voice called from beneath the great furry mass. "What is all this? Where am I?"

A gray head popped up behind the huge ferret's form. It was Mother Duck. She frowned.

"This looks an awful lot like Vushta. Why would I come to Vushta?"

Nobody answered her, save for those few wizards still sneezing.

"Smelly place," Mother Duck grumped. "Noisy, too. It's no wonder everybody has a cold. Does anyone know the way to the Eastern Kingdoms?"

Everyone who was capable of it pointed east.

"What am I doing, wandering around like this? I hope I'm not getting too old. And *Vushta*?" She made a face. "Next thing you know, I'll wind up straying into those dreadful Western Kingdoms." She waved vaguely at the crowd around her. "Excuse me, but there's no place like home." And with that, she wandered back in the general direction of her domain.

"Doom," Hendrek remarked when the old lady had passed out of sight. "She was about to attack us, and make Vushta part of her kingdom."

"Then," Norei added from Hendrek's side, "as she was calling forth all the sorcery at her command, you showed up."

"Indeed?" Ebenezum replied. "It's no wonder, then. Instead of the sorceries she desired, she was overcome by an enchanted ferret. And what an enchanted ferret! An overload of that sort would undo anyone in the magical arts."

"Oops!" Richard the giant added in wonder. "So she's gone?"

"It would appear so," the wizard agreed.

The Seven Other Dwarves cheered along.

"Hi hun, hi hun,
    Then that must mean we've won!"

"That's right!" Tap pulled at my pants leg. "That means His Brownieship is bound to take me back! Doesn't it?"

"Indeed," my master answered. "At least Mother Duck is no longer a threat. But what of the Netherhells?"

I took a moment to explain what Mother Duck had done to the demon's Conquest by Committee.

"Really?" the wizard replied, a certain admiration in his voice. "Then perhaps we will have a chance to fix the damage done to Vushta before the Netherhells can regroup."

A gruff voice came from the crowd, accompanied by Rapid drumbeats.

"Interject!"

The former Grand Hoohah stepped forward. Brax the salesdemon was only half a pace behind.

> "Guxx Unfufadoo, relieved demon,
> Glad he is that you've defeated
> Mother Duck, and says those demons
> Down below are ripe for conquest!"

"That's right!" Brax added. "Guxx and I are going back to the Netherhells to take over again!"

"Doom," Hendrek remarked. "All by yourselves?"

"Contradict!" Guxx exclaimed. Brax beat his rhythm.

> "Guxx Unfufadoo, vengeful demon,
> Has the claws so right for tearing;
> Has the muscles strong for rending;
> Thinks that these will do quite nicely!"

No one disagreed with the demon, who only sneezed slightly at his rhyme.

"So I guess we'll be on our way!" Brax called to the rest of us. "Now there's one thing I want you all to consider carefully: This is your last chance to buy a really high-quality used weapon, just in case, shall we say, that we end up on opposite sides."

There were no takers here, either.

"Conquer!" Guxx announced. He marched off with Brax beating the drum behind him.

"Indeed," Ebenezum mused with a tug of his beard. "Things seem simpler hereabouts since the last time I was in the neighborhood. Perhaps now we can get around to curing the wizards."

"And get everything back to normal?" I asked.

"Yes, Wuntvor," Norei said as she approached me. "I'm glad to have you back."

"So everything's all right?" Hubert cheered, releasing a substantial quantity of smoke. "Alea! Let's do a snappy musical number in celebration."

The damsel stepped forward from the crowd, but she was frowning. "Musical number? Look, Hubie, I've been meaning to talk to you in private—" her voice died, her hands fluttering at her sides. She paused, then sighed. "Well, I suppose I could do it, if it's okay with my new partner."

"New partner?" the dragon yelped in astonishment.

The damsel looked down at her dancing-slippered feet. "Well, you know, you were gone for an awful long time. And I wasn't sure you were ever coming back. I mean, a girl's got to eat!"

"But Alea!" Hubert protested. "Who could take the place of a dragon?"

"Oops," Richard commented.

Alea smiled encouragingly up at the giant. "Take it, Richard! Let's show them our stuff!"

And the giant and Alea sang together:

"Hey, we've got something
    You can really dig;
    When we do a big show,
    It's really big!
    All of Vushta is in a whirl
    For a giant and a girl!"

Alea pirouetted prettily as Richard stomped half a dozen foothills behind her.

"I thought Damsel and Dragon was as bad as this sort of thing could get," Snarks whispered. "I was wrong."

"Doom," Hendrek agreed in an equally hushed tone, glancing up at the rampaging giant. "But who's going to criticize them?"

Snorphosio the wizard ran into our midst.

"The Dealer of Death!" he cried with uncharacteristic abruptness. "He has revived!"

And the Dealer was right behind him. The well-muscled assassin smiled.

"Not only revived," he murmured pleasantly, "but ready to strangle. Show me those wild pigs!"

"How could she?" Hubert moaned overhead. "I do admit their act has a certain novelty value when considered on a very large scale, but still, what's a dragon to do?"

A furry fellow in a green hat tugged at the dragon's tail. "I say, big guy. Have you ever considered how unique your act might be with the assistance of a talented talking wolf?"

And I heard another, magnificently modulated voice from the rear of the crowd:

"My lap has returned." The unicorn sighed musically. "I am content."

"And Wuntie?" Alea fluttered her eyelashes prettily. "When you have a chance, we have all sorts of catching up to do!"

Norei squeezed my arm, somehow managing to drag me in her direction. "I guess you are right, Wuntvor. Everything is back to normal."

"Indeed," my master added, "and we must get back to work."

Arm in arm, Norei and I followed my master, the great wizard Ebenezum, back toward the university library. The sun was bright overhead, and the air had the crisp edge of early fall. I felt a spring in my step, brought about by being back among those whom I loved best, and on the verge of solving all our problems.

"EEEP!" the fifty-foot-high ferret called as it happily trundled after us.

I squeezed Norei's hand. I mean, what could possibly go wrong now?

A selection of bestsellers
from Headline

FICTION

THE MASK	Dean R Koontz	£3.50 ☐
ROWAN'S MILL	Elizabeth Walker	£3.99 ☐
MONEY FOR NOTHING	John Harman	£3.99 ☐
RICOCHET	Ovid Demaris	£3.50 ☐
SHE GOES TO WAR	Edith Pargeter	£3.50 ☐
CLOSE-UP ON DEATH	Maureen O'Brien	£2.99 ☐

NON-FICTION

GOOD HOUSEKEEPING EATING FOR A HEALTHY HEART	Coronary Prevention Group	£3.99 ☐
THE ALIEN'S DICTIONARY	David Hallamshire	£2.99 ☐

SCIENCE FICTION AND FANTASY

THE FIRE SWORD	Adrienne Martine-Barnes	£3.99 ☐
SHADOWS OF THE WHITE SUN	Raymond Harris	£2.99 ☐
AN EXCESS OF ENCHANTMENTS	Craig Shaw Gardner	£2.99 ☐
MOON DREAMS	Brad Strickland	£3.50 ☐

All Headline books are available at your local bookshop or newsagent, or can be ordered direct from the publisher. Just tick the titles you want and fill in the form below. Prices and availability subject to change without notice.

Headline Book Publishing PLC, Cash Sales Department, PO Box 11, Falmouth, Cornwall, TR10 9EN, England.

Please enclose a cheque or postal order to the value of the cover price and allow the following for postage and packing:
UK: 60p for the first book, 25p for the second book and 15p for each additional book ordered up to a maximum charge of £1.90
BFPO: 60p for the first book, 25p for the second book and 15p per copy for the next seven books, thereafter 9p per book
OVERSEAS & EIRE: £1.25 for the first book, 75p for the second book and 28p for each subsequent book.

Name ....

Address ....

....

....